M000318148

STOWE AWAY

A CANADIAN WEREWOLF NOVELLA

MARK LESLIE

Stark Publishing

STARK
PUBLISHING

Stark Publishing
Waterloo, ON
www.markleslie.ca

Publisher's Note: This is a work of fiction. Names, characters, places, and incidents are a product of the author's imagination. Real locales and public and celebrity names are sometimes used for atmospheric purposes. Any resemblance to actual people, living or dead, or to businesses, companies, events, institutions, or locales is either completely coincidental or is used in a completely fictional manner.

Book Layout © 2014 BookDesignTemplates.com
Cover Design © 2020 Juan Padron

Stowe Away / Mark Leslie. -- 1st ed.
Hardcover ISBN: 978-1-989351-13-0
Trade Paperback Print ISBN: 978-1-989351-12-3
eBook ISBN: 978-1-989351-14-7
Audiobook ISBN: 978-1-989351-15-4

First paper printing July 2020

For Deanna and Jamie.
Thank you for the prompt that led to this story.

Table of Contents

STOWE AWAY

Friday July 31, 2015

5:54 AM

YOU'D THINK, AFTER all this time, that I'd be used to it.

But no matter how many times I wake up naked, with my body mostly hidden away in some sort of greenery and no memory of the previous night or how I got there, it is still a startling way to begin my day.

Since I have no conscious memory of the change between man and wolf, I have to rely on how Gail, my closest friend, has described it. She says it looks like a cross between an episode of violent childbirth and the Wicked Witch of the West melting as, over the space of about sixty seconds, I change from a six-foot-two, two-hundred-pound human into a one-hundred-pound, six-foot-long grey wolf.

The memory loss is likely a sanity-preserving side effect of the terrifying physical transmogrification.

I imagine these mornings are similar to what career drunks or drug addicts might experience waking up in strange places every morning, those first few confusing seconds at least. For me it's a little different. Sadly, there's no manual, no *Werewolves for Dummies* book to help explain my specific situation or predicament. But I have, at least, established a bit of a routine, or a process, of dealing with the cycles of the wolf I experience every month. I tend to plan out most of my transformations in the large green space of southern Central Park in Manhattan, and have the presence of mind to hide a change of clothes for the next day.

Where else, after all, can a werewolf safely make his change in such a large metropolis?

~

As I sit up and pay attention to my surroundings, I take in the sights, sounds, and smells and recognize the part of the park where I am, an area known as the Ramble, across the Lake from Strawberry Fields, the well-visited memorial to John Lennon.

One of my usual clothes-stash areas is just a few meters north of Bow Bridge. I have a half-dozen stash areas. Sometimes a crafty homeless person comes across one of them, or a small animal tears the bag apart to use some of the clothes for nesting material.

I listen for anyone nearby.

And, despite being male, listening is something I do extremely well. Or at least, in an enhanced way. When in human form, I retain heightened senses, extraordinary strength, and a super-charged immune system. Those side-effects come in extremely handy.

The closest human-generated sound is a pair of joggers on the other side of the Loeb Boathouse about a quarter of a mile across the lake. Dozens of birds are singing a multitude of beautiful choruses and zipping about in the treetops. There's a rabbit about twenty feet or so north of me that pauses in its shuffling and tenses into high alert the moment I started to stand up. And a few feet to my left, a squirrel is scurrying up a tree.

But, other than that, I'm alone. It takes me less than a minute to make my way to the fortunately unmolested stash of clothes, tucked in a small crevasse between the thick roots of a tree trunk.

One can't simply walk down 5th Avenue butt naked, after all.

I pull the day's ensemble—a cheap pair of track pants, a t-shirt and sneakers—out of their plastic bag, a bit damp from the rain and heavy fog yesterday afternoon.

At least I have clothes.

As I pull the pants on, I cringe slightly at the dampness. Once I have them on, I see a fully soaked spot about two inches wide, located dead center at my crotch. Great. The wet spot, which, on the grey material is as subtle as a slap in the face with a trout, makes me look like I've wet myself.

When I finish dressing, I head over to the trail, cross Bow Bridge, then head south through the park. There's something calming and peaceful about being in the park this early, before it starts to fill with local joggers and dog walkers, and later on with tourists. I quite relish this part of my walk. It's a great chance to recharge and refresh the mind, preparing me for a decent hour or two of writing.

My writing time will be limited this morning because of my plans to meet Gail, the only woman I've ever loved or trusted with the truth of my condition, at eight a.m. for breakfast. We're meeting at a café in the East Village not far from Gail's metaphysical supply store, *Enchanting Magic*. Gail has owned the shop for more than a decade. She has three staff members who work for her, but she regularly likes to be the one to open the shop, which she does at eleven a.m. most weekdays. It is typically quiet there until mid-afternoon.

The fifteen-minute walk to The Algonquin Hotel, which is my full-time residence, is a chance for me to contemplate the next scene in the Maxwell Bronte novel that I'm working on. Although, to be honest, picturing Gail's smile across the diner table from me keeps interrupting my thoughts.

Gail and I had something truly special once. A love like nothing I had ever experienced before. And I screwed that up. But at least we are friends, dear friends. Despite the fact I wish there could be more, despite the fact I can sense she does too, though she isn't able to be more than friends right now. She is still coming to terms with recently finding out her ex-fiancé was an underworld criminal. And I have no intension of pushing her. So I'll be there for her as a friend, and I'll wait patiently until she is ready, the way she patiently attends to me when I am forced to spend the night as a wolf when I'm trapped inside.

But in the meantime, I really need to get a new hobby. Something to stop me from obsessing over her.

"We're good friends," I mutter as I leave the park on my way to cross West 59th Street. "We're good friends." It's a mantra I have to keep repeating to myself.

"Buddy, we just met," says a gruff male voice off to my left. "How about you buy me a coffee and at least ask me my name before we get that intimate?"

I look over to my left to see a homeless guy leaning against the low brick wall at the edge of Central Park. He looks like he is in his mid-sixties, with weathered, sun-baked and leathery skin, smelling of sweat from wearing the same clothes for weeks. He has a hearty and healthy heartbeat, and, obviously, a good sense of humor and a solid mind.

I smile at him as I pause on the sidewalk, turn towards him, and pat at the tops of my legs where pockets would be if I had any. "Wish I could, my friend. Afraid I'm fresh out at the moment. I'm Michael."

"S'all good," he says. "You can call me Saul."

"Good to meet you, Saul. We'll have to take a rain check on that coffee, okay?"

"Sounds good," Saul says. Then he notices the wet spot on the front of my pants. "Tell you what, Michael. If you come into any dough, maybe you should invest in a pair of Depends. Sound like a plan?"

I laugh, looking down at the still obvious blotch of dark wetness.

"It's a marvelous plan," I tell him, and then turn to continue my walk.

"You have yourself a good day, Michael," he says. "May the wind be ever at your back."

"You too, Saul." I call over my shoulder.

Over the years my extrasensory abilities have allowed me the chance to really understand the unique comraderies of the people of this city, all of them—from the ones living in the richest towers to the ones who struggle to find a spot to sleep at night. On the surface, the Big Apple can appear cold and harsh. But underneath, it's no different than any other city or town. Sure, there are jerks. But there's also some decent heart.

I manage to make it back to the hotel without anyone else making commentary about the wet spot across my crotch. That's not to say people don't notice. I can sense and scent their reactions. I often wonder if the unspoken judgements we hold against strangers could sometimes be harsher than words spoken in truth.

I make it up to my room and am greeted by a blinking light on my phone. There is a voicemail waiting for me.

The first message is from Gail at 9:20 p.m. last night.

"Hi Michael. It's me," the message says. "Just letting you know that I won't be able to meet you for breakfast in the morning. I'm on my way to the airport to catch a flight to Vermont. It's my Uncle Albert. He had a stroke. I'm grabbing the first flight. I'll let you know when I get in."

The devastation in her voice is intense. Uncle Albert wasn't just a favorite uncle to Gail. He was, and still is, a father figure to her. He practically raised her.

The next message is also from Gail. It came in at 3:41 a.m.

"Hi Michael. I'm at the University of Vermont Medical Center in Burlington. I'm with Uncle Albert. He's not doing well. He's still unconscious and his vital signs are weak."

I can almost smell the fear and helplessness in her voice.

The third message from Gail came at 5:01 a.m.

"There's been no change. I don't know," her voice breaks and she lets out a stifled sob, "I don't know what I would do without him, Michael." There is a long pause while she struggles to gain some composure. "Also, my phone is down to one percent battery. I didn't pack a charging cable, so I likely won't be able to call again for a while. I will when I can."

Uncle Albert is well beyond a favourite uncle and mentor; he's the one person in the family she could count on for support and guidance when things went south for her and she stumbled in her teen years. He is the inspiration and the support she counts on in order to pick herself back up, to keep going any time she feels herself slipping. His presence, his love, and his compassion were among the main reasons she didn't take her own life when she was in her darkest, weakest moment. Uncle Albert is the one person she can count on to be there for her when she needs it the most.

The immediacy of the moment hit me hard. I understand how alone, how vulnerable, how terrified Gail must feel.

I needed to get to Vermont.

11:52 AM

AS THE TRAIN left the Bronx northward on the bridge over Pelham Bay, I peered out the window on my right. I got a glimpse of the most rural landscape I had seen in several years. If I'd been looking in the opposite direction, I would have still seen the signs of the city, urban landscape and tall buildings jutting upwards.

New York has plenty of green spaces and beautiful landscapes. But there was a greater sense of an open landscape here that I reveled in as we began the journey out of the city and the rural landscape of New York State began to reveal itself. Prior to moving to Manhattan more than ten years ago, I'd lived in a small town in Ontario, Canada. My back yard had been wilderness. And, as the greener, more rural landscape rolled past, I felt an odd sense of comfort, despite the anxiety that compelled me to be on this trip.

I had to get to Gail. She needed a friend now more than ever.

A flight to Burlington, Vermont, would have been about an hour. But I couldn't do that. I became a permanent resident of the US more than six years ago and am a fully-fledged dual US and Canadian citizen. But I had let my passports expire, and, living in a city with a world-class public transit system and more taxis than you can shake a stick at, I had never bothered to get a driver's licence for the State of New York. I couldn't even imagine trying to learn how to drive in a big city like that. I hadn't been much of a driver before, either, apart from the occasional tractor, quad or snow machine in the rural north.

With a quick call to Mack, my literary agent, I'm sure there would have been a way to fly, even with an expired ID. But I was still behind on my latest deadline, and wasn't about to reach out to him and provoke his wraith.

So I purchased the train ticket.

The Vermonter train left Pennsylvania Station at 11:30 a.m. and performed nineteen stops on its way to Essex, Vermont, in just under nine hours. From there, I'd take a transfer to an Amtrak bound for Burlington, where Gail's uncle was in the hospital.

The only clincher in this plan was the fact that the train arrived in Essex Junction at 8:18 p.m. And, according to a quick Google search, sunset in that county in Vermont would take place at 8:17 p.m. during a full moon. Which meant my transformation into wolf form would be happening as we pulled into our last stop. And I had no plan for how to handle that.

So, I did what I often do. I acted first, determined that I would figure something out along the way.

It's how I ended up in New York, after all. Hitchhiking into the city with a dream of fulfilling my dream of being a writer.

Yep, I often acted the way that I wrote. A man with a basic plan or idea; a rough outline, and the belief that I'd figure it out somewhere along the way.

It seemed to work out okay for my novels.

And, so far, it served me well on the life journey.

So I wasn't as nervous as I likely should have been.

After all, I had eight hours to figure it all out.

As I returned to gazing out the window at the landscape, I kept experiencing fleeting memories of the night before as experienced by the wolf-part of my mind.

Running through the underbrush of the forest-laden hills of Central Park, and the accompanying sense of pure unadulterated joy.

The satisfaction of quenching a deep thirst by lapping at the cool water at the edge of a lake.

Pausing to sniff the air, aware of the nearby sound of a human shuffling slowly down a trail just a few yards away, and, at the same time, the wail of a siren echoing from somewhere behind the safety of the park.

Clips and short memories of various moments are pretty typical of most of my nights as a wolf. I have often wondered if my wolf form has visions of the things I have done during the previous day, or any idea that it has another form as a human.

The retrospective clips of the night before were interspersed with flashes of the memory of Gail's cool-green eyes staring back into mine on the night of our first date, of the intensity of her passion in those same eyes when we were in the clenches of making love.

Similar to the fleeting glimpses of my experiences as a wolf, those special memories of moments with Gail were distant, and further muted over time.

Both were similar in their almost dream-like existence.

Before leaving, I had tried to call Gail several times. It kept going straight to her voice mail, which suggested that her phone was still dead. I left a couple of messages. One to let her know I got her message and was planning on coming to be with her. A second one to let her know I had booked a train ticket and was on my way up there.

I hadn't bothered leaving any other messages before rushing to the train station. I instinctively reached down to pat my pocket for my mobile phone, thinking I should try to reach out and call Gail, then remembered I had de-cided to leave it at home. I don't like having things on me that I could easily lose track of when in wolf form. All I had with me was a backpack filled with a few changes of clothes, minimal toiletries, and a thin wallet with some cash and the single credit card I had used to purchase the train ticket online with.

As the countryside became more rural outside the train window, I was reminded of the encroaching dead-line to figure out a proper plan on what I was going to do when the clock struck "moon-rise" and I began to turn into the proverbial pumpkin.

I needed to figure out a plan.

1:41 PM

I WOKE UP as the train was pulling out of New Haven, Connecticut. There was something about the gentle and rhythmic pulse of the train that had coaxed me into sleep. Yes, even with the concern over Gail as well as my worry over needing to figure out a solution before the train arrived in Essex.

While my supernaturally enhanced strength and senses were heightened during my monthly wolf cycles, I was also occasionally overcome with fatigue when in human form, perhaps because my human mind didn't get the sleep needed for a properly functioning, average adult.

Based on where we were, I figured I had gotten a good solid hour and a half of sleep. I also figured I should stop procrastinating and get my butt into gear figuring out a plan. I got up from my seat and started to walk towards the front of the train. I wanted to figure out the layout of the train, and what sorts of cars it contained. Perhaps there would be a useful hiding spot I could use. Trying to find a hiding spot inside an enclosed space for a wild animal might seem like a preposterous idea, like taking one's bull into a china shop, but it had worked. At least a few times.

Gail, who'd been with me for most of those times, explained that it appeared my wolfish form recognized the danger that came with being discovered. Perhaps it was instinct; perhaps an indication of some of my human consciousness leaking through. I did have fleeting memories of being in wolf form in an enclosed space while Gail was with me. Those snippets came with an overwhelming feeling of what I can only describe, in human terms, as trust, love, and respect.

It's easy for me to understand how any mammal, human or otherwise, could have those feelings for Gail; she has a presence and energy that immediately commands respect and trust; the love, I imagine, is likely a side-effect of the human blood pulsing through my wolf form.

I made my way from the coach train car I had been sitting in and moved forward into the next one, which was a lounge. A few people were relaxing there, enjoying a coffee and seats that faced the windows. The car after that was the dining car, where the overwhelming smells of food almost changed the course of my mission. Sure, I had eaten a hearty breakfast, but I could certainly use more food. The calories I burned transforming from human to wolf form and then back again were substantial. I picked up my pace to get the dining car behind me.

As I moved onto the next car, a sleeper, I took note of the indicators of the bunks. So far, all of them were occupied except one. I had intended to attempt to try to open the unoccupied one, but a man entered from the car in front, so I just kept walking.

The man, who had the large, muscular frame of a body builder and a pencil-thin black moustache, looked to be in his mid-twenties. He smelled of garlic and the woody oak scent of whisky, with a skunky base of pot. I sensed heightened anger, both in his scent and in the strong and heightened beat of his heart, as he moved quickly and purposely through the car and toward me. The anger wasn't directed at me but on something else. Something he seemed to be desperately searching for—and extremely angry about.

My instincts suggested it was most likely a partner he had had a falling out with. His eyes kept moving from me to the doors of the sleeper car rooms, the way a hungry canine might eye dog treats on the floor. As we passed one another, both squeezing to get by in the confined space, he smiled at me, one of those smiles that causes the lips to form the proper shape but fails to make it to the eyes. His glance at me also came with an air of annoyance, like I was a mosquito buzzing around his ear. I wondered who had pissed in his cornflakes.

I didn't, of course, have to wonder long.

I made my way through the sleeper car. Cornflake Guy exited into the dining car behind me. At the far end of the car, I picked up a distinct scent from the room marked as unoccupied.

I recognized the scent immediately: a woman filled with absolute fear.

I had first picked up on it going down the escalator to the train at Penn Station. The odor had been pervasive as I descended to the track level. It had been from someone who had moved through the same space only a minute or so before me, and the anxiety and fear was so palpable to me that it stuck in my mind, although I hadn't been able to follow it at the time.

A colleague of mine, Barney, who manages a bookshop on the upper East Side, once explained it to me. Having been a bookseller for more than thirty years, Barney couldn't not notice a reader. It could be someone reading a book on a park bench, carrying a paperback or a Kindle eReader. Wherever Barney looked, readers jumped out at him.

He couldn't not see them; couldn't not notice them.

It was the same for me.

Me, I couldn't not sense those who needed help.

I had lived most of my life with an underlying, Stan Lee-infused philosophy of power and responsibility. Growing up on a steady diet of Spider-Man comic books, I had a sense of wanting to use my powers to help others in any way I could.

As a wolf, picking up on scents of those who might need help had become second nature to me.

I couldn't detect the woman when I was boarding the train, but her scent had stood out. And now it was far more intense than it had been at the train station.

The woman was inside the bunk to my right. I could hear the rapid beating of her heart and the short, quick breaths she was taking in an attempt to be as quiet as possible. She was fearful for her life.

I looked back to ensure that Cornflake hadn't returned, then opened the door.

The woman's anxiety ratcheted up all the way to eleven as her "fight or flight" mode shifted to attack mode.

The room was small, with two large armchair seats across from one another at the window, and a mirror and a sink to the left. The upper bunk was still pushed all the way to the ceiling. Her scent was coming from above and almost behind me. There must be some sort of luggage storage compartment above the door where she was tucked away.

"It's okay," I said in a voice that was almost a whisper as I slowly inched my way into the room. "I'm not here to hurt you. I know you're scared."

A voice came over the train's PA system as the train began to noticeably slow down. "Meriden is the next stop. We are arriving in Meriden."

Her fight or flight response kicked up even higher. Either this was her stop, or she was calculating her chances of being able to get away from me and escape off the train once it came to a stop.

"Is this your stop? Do you need to get off here?"

There was no answer. But her breathing changed subtly, as if she had opened her mouth and considered speaking.

"Listen, I know you are hiding from someone and I won't let them find you. I promise."

The train was beginning to slow down as it pulled into the station at Meriden.

"My name is Michael Andrews. I'm on my way to Burlington, Vermont, to visit a friend whose uncle is ill. I'm a writer. I promise I mean you no harm, and only want to help you stay away from whoever it is you are hiding from."

Her heartbeat jumped a split second after I said my name. Then her anxiety changed to a scent that included a sense of wonderment.

I could hear her drawing in a deep breath.

Muffled, almost as if from behind a wall, she said, "*No way!*" Her voice sounded young.

I chuckled. "What? Are you heading to Burlington to see a sick friend too?"

"Are you really Michael Andrews? The author of *Print of the Predator*? *Tome of Terror*? The guy who created Maxwell Bronte? You've got to be freakin' kidding me!" She giggled.

As a writer, I was used to most people not recognizing me, despite the fact that a Hollywood movie starring Ryan Gosling had been made from one of my novels. I had been a multi-time *New York Times* bestselling author, had been on *Late Night with David Letterman*, had been featured in hundreds of newspapers and magazines around the world, and my book signings commanded long lines. But the average person has no idea who I am.

So it was still rare for anybody to recognize my name.

"Uh, yeah. That's me."

"*The* Michael Andrews?" she said, her voice and scent filled with a slight bit of incredulousness.

"In the flesh."

"No way!"

"*Waaaaay*," I said.

She giggled again.

The train came to a complete stop. The male voice over the PA system said, "Meriden Station. This stop is Meriden Station."

"Listen." I said. "I'm stepping all the way inside so I can close the door. I don't want whoever you're hiding from to know you're here. Is that okay?"

Her anxiety raced up again. "Y-yeah," she said. "Okay."

"You don't need to get off at this stop, do you?"

"No," she said. "This isn't my stop."

"Okay. I'm closing the door." I closed it, then turned down the latch to lock it. "It's locked. They won't find you." I paused, thinking about Cornflake, about the purposeful way he had been storming through the car, his eyes darting to the doors on each side. He had been angry and searching. I now knew who he was searching for. "*He* won't find you."

"How did you know I was hiding from a man?"

"I think I saw him. Tall. Muscles on top of muscles. Thin moustache. Is that him?"

Her fear shot up again. I didn't have to hear her confirmation to know I was right.

"Yes," she said in a hoarse whisper. "That's him. Where is he?"

"I just passed him in the hall outside. He was—"

The PA told us that the train was now on its way again as the train began its crawl out of the station.

I continued, "He was heading toward the back of the train. But I could tell he was looking for something, or someone. He was moving with purpose and—"

The sound of the door between the railcars creaking open came with the return of his fresh scent. I stopped. "Don't move. He's coming back."

The door in the dining car opened. Cornflake's scent began moving back in our direction. As I stood facing the door, I could hear Cornflake's footsteps as he moved onto the car, the sound of the door to the car closing behind him, smell his anger and determination.

This time, he was pausing to check the doors as he moved through the car.

The curtain over the window in our door was closed. The one over the small window beside it was mostly closed, but the Velcro tab wasn't attached, leaving a half-inch crack.

As Cornflake neared our room, he spotted me looking out from the crack in the curtains. We made eye contact for the briefest moment. His scent and heartbeat gave away his surprise at being caught. He stopped midway through the motion of reaching for our door latch, but stopped and immediately shuffled past.

A few doors down he tried the latches again, then made his way to the end of the car and exited through the door there.

"Okay," I said. "He's gone."

Her heartbeat slowed from the race it had been on and her fear abated a little.

"Who is he?" I asked.

Her head popped over the edge of the small open luggage compartment above me as she looked down. She was young, very pretty. Wavy, light-blonde hair. Piercing blue eyes. She looked maybe sixteen or seventeen, but the tone and intonation of her voice gave her away as someone a lot younger.

"No way," she said, staring at me with wide eyes. "You really are Michael Andrews."

"Who is he?" I asked again. "That guy stalking around out there."

"Can I climb down?" she asked. "It's really cramped up here."

"Yeah," I said, stepping back to stand in front of the two seats facing one another near the window. "Do you need help?"

"I'm good." She wiggled out of the luggage compartment and used the steps designed into the sink and toilet to make her way down. She was slim but quite tall; watching her lanky body come out of that tight luggage storage space over the door was akin to watching clown after clown pile out of one of those tiny cars at the circus.

She stepped down. She was almost as tall as I was. I stepped back as much as I could, not that there was much space for two people standing in that tight area. She let out a sigh of relief and reached down to rub the backs of her legs. "My legs were getting so cramped up there."

Suddenly her blue eyes couldn't leave mine. "Oh my God, I can't believe I'm meeting *the* Michael Andrews. I've read all of your novels. I love them. I've read all of your books. Even the short story collection. I know that the reviewers didn't like it, but I thought it was fascinating to get to read stories that weren't about Maxwell Bronte. I thought—"

"Thank you. I am truly honored," I said, putting out my hand. "But you've got one up on me. You know I'm Michael Andrews. But I don't know your name."

She took my hand and gave it a firm shake. The confidence and strength in that handshake again made me think she might be an older teenager. But I doubted she was. Something about her speech, her mannerisms, even her pulse rate, suggested someone younger. Much younger.

"I'm Bridget." She said. "Bridget Wells."

"Pleased to meet you, Bridget."

"My friends call me Bridge," she said. "I've read all your books. Read so many articles about you and interviews. I feel like I know you. Call me Bridge."

"Pleased to meet you, Bridge. There's not a lot of room in here," I said. "Why don't we take a seat?" I inched my way to the one chair on my right.

She smiled and plopped into the chair across from me.

"Who is that guy?" I asked.

Her heart began to race again, there was a sour scent of fear. "I've read all of your books. I wanted to ask if you'll be putting out any more story collections like that last one."

I smiled. "Thank you. I'm honored."

She smiled, and I could tell she thought she had again successfully steered the conversation away from having to answer.

"Who *is* he, Bridge?" I repeated.

"Bruce," she said, letting out a long breath. "His name is Bruce. He's a friend of my dad. He was younger than most of them. And I thought he was cute, too. We used to talk about stuff together. I thought he was cool. But last night, that changed. He's not cool. He...he's a pig."

I just listened. I knew there was more coming as she took in another long breath.

"My Dad was having a party. He has lots of parties. Lots of people. Everyone was drinking, smoking up. And dancing. I was standing in the hallway watching them. Bruce saw me and asked me to dance. I love dancing, and Bruce and I always got along. We enjoyed playing the same video games, talking about the same movies. So I joined in. Everyone was laughing, having a good time. Then, a few minutes later when I was in the kitchen getting a soda from the fridge, Bruce came up behind me, put his hand around my waist, turned me around. He was drunk. I could smell the booze and the pot on his breath. Then he leaned in and kissed me."

Bridge pauses and looks out the window and takes a deep breath before continuing.

"I was shocked. It happened so fast I didn't know what was happening. I tried to back away, but the open fridge door was behind me, so I bumped into it. Bruce kissed me again. And he put his tongue in my mouth and moved his hand lower, over my butt. I could taste the alcohol, the weed from his tongue. Disgusting."

"Cheryl steps into the kitchen then. She's another friend of my dad. She's a lot older. 'What are you doing?' she says.

"Bruce steps back and just smiles at Cheryl. 'Nothing.'

"'Bruce,' Cheryl says. 'She's only a kid.'

"'We were just goofing around,' Bruce says. 'She said she wanted to learn how to kiss. I was helping her out.'

"Cheryl walks over to me and asks if that's true. Bruce is staring daggers at me. 'Yeah,' I say. I take a can of orange soda out of the fridge, open it and drink some, no big deal.

"'Cheryl leans toward me and I can tell she's high. She whispers, 'Might as well learn from the best. He is one hell of a kisser.' She steps over to Bruce, slaps his butt, then puts her arms around him and says, 'It's been a while since I've had a kissing lesson, honeybun.'

"Bruce and Cheryl start making out. I go to the washroom, and I throw up. The orange soda I just had comes out. That makes me even more sick."

She began to gasp for breath, as if re-experiencing the nausea, then quietly shook her head. For a moment she was unable to speak

"I stay in the washroom for a long time. I can't believe what just happened. Or how stupid I was. But thinking about what Bruce did is what makes me sick again. Only nothing comes out. I was so stupid."

I said, "You did nothing wrong, Bridge."

She remained quiet. Her heartbeat was beating a mile a minute.

"How old are you, Bridge?"

"Thirteen." Her eyes filled with tears. "I'd only ever kissed a boy once, at summer camp. Last summer. We were playing spin-the-bottle. I had a huge crush on him. It was a quick peck on the lips. But with Bruce it was hard and my lips hurt. His breath was horrible. The tongue! It was disgusting."

I am feeling disgusted myself. Anger and resentment at the asshole I'd seen in the hallway. Frustration that this innocent child had something like this forced on her. I was ready to kill the man. I had to take a deep breath.

"That's because it wasn't a kiss, Bridge. He was assaulting you. He had no right to do that to you."

"But instead of telling Cheryl when I had the chance, I helped him cover it up."

"You did nothing wrong."

"Oh yeah?" Tears started streaming down her face. "Then why didn't my dad believe me? When I was sitting in the washroom, I was scared Bruce was going to do something like that again. So I washed my face, used mouthwash to rinse my mouth, and went out to the living room to tell my dad. He was dancing with a bunch of other friends. I pulled him into the kitchen.

"When I told him he just stood there looking at me like he didn't know what I was saying. He was high and drunk.

"But before he could say anything, Bruce and Cheryl walked in, arm in arm.

"'Bruce,' my dad says. 'Is this true? Did you just kiss Bridget in the kitchen?'

"Cheryl says, 'I was there when it happened. She wanted to know how to kiss. Bruce said no but she kept bugging him.'

"My dad turns to me, and do you know what he says? He says: 'Why would you make something like that up about my friend?'

"Then the three of them laughed about the wild imagination of teenagers, lit up another joint to share, and moved off to the living room together.

"My Dad didn't believe me. But then Cheryl says I was asking for it. I know she wasn't even there when it started, but I can't help second-guessing myself. Maybe I remembered it wrong. Maybe I was acting in a way with Bruce that brought him on. Maybe I *was* flirting with him. I did like hanging out with him.

"I know what I thought happened. But I don't know what to believe."

Bridge dropped her face into her hands.

I sat silently across from her, forcing myself not to touch her. The last thing she needed was to worry about a stranger getting too close for comfort.

Finally, she lifted her head up and looked up at me. "I'm sorry. I couldn't help crying. I know I sound like a baby. But I couldn't help it."

"It's okay. You have nothing to apologize for. Bridge, you did nothing wrong. This was something uninvited, unwelcomed, unwanted, that happened to you. But you have to tell me, because I don't understand. How did you get here?"

"Afterwards, I wandered around the party. Bruce and Cheryl went into my dad's bedroom. I decided to go to sleep. But I couldn't sleep. The music and the voices, the shouting, the singing, all of it was too loud. And I could hear Bruce and Cheryl doing it. They were really loud. I went to the washroom and tried to throw up but there was nothing more to come out. I went back to my bedroom, put on my headphones and played some music to drown out all the noise.

"I woke up later. It was quiet. The partying was over. Then I look over and see Bruce standing on the side of my bed.

"He's naked. And...um. *Up.*

"'Bridget,' he whispers. 'We aren't finished, you and me. I've seen the way you look at me. I know you want me. I'm here to teach you more. I'm here to help you become the woman I know you want to be.'

"He pulls the blankets off of me, then he puts one knee onto the bed and grabs on to my shoulder.

"'No,' I say.

"He says, 'Don't be like that. You know you want it. I could see it in your eyes. You want a taste of old Brucey.'

"I don't know what to do. He pushes me onto my back. He's so strong and I can't move at all. Then he lifts one leg over to climb on top of me.

"I jab up with my knee as hard as I can. I knee him right between the legs. He gasps and lets go of my shoulder. I knee him between the legs again. Even harder. He doesn't move. I shove him off the bed. He must have passed out from the pain, because he doesn't get up.

"I get out of bed and grab the jeans and t-shirt I was wearing before bed. I grab some cash and a Metro card I left on top of my dresser and shove them into my pocket. But my phone is on the nightstand on the far side of the bed, right beside Bruce.

"I start to walk over to grab it, but he's moaning and getting to his knees. I give up on the phone and open the door to leave and I hear him hiss behind me.

"'You little bitch,' he says. 'I was going to be gentle with you. But not now. Now I'm going to fuck you so hard. Because I can tell you like it rough.' I slam the door behind me. I run down the stairs to the street and keep running. I don't know what I'm doing. Finally I just stand there.

"I hear him. He's calling my name. Then he spots me. He's about a block away. He yells that he needs to talk to me. But I know that's not what he wants.

"I run to the nearest Metro station and take the next train, hoping he doesn't get there before it leaves. I go to Manhattan. The only thing I can think of is to get to Pennsylvania Station so I can take the train to Vermont. My mom and I moved there when I was nine. I'm only in New York to spend the summer with Dad.

"As I'm looking out at the tracks, I see Bruce. He's all the way on the other side of the train platform coming down the escalator. He's looking right at me.

"I get up from my seat and start looking for somewhere to hide. This was the only place I could think of. He's going to catch me. I'm so stupid."

She dropped her face back down into her palms.

"I'm so sorry, Bridge," I said.

Like a little kid, she put her arms out for a hug. I put both arms around her and just held her quietly for a moment while she cried, almost soundlessly.

I whispered to her, "I won't let him get close to you. I will not let him hurt you. And I'll make sure you make it to your mom safely."

She stopped crying and looked up into my eyes.

"Thank you."

In her eyes as well as in the emotions I could smell, was her complete and unadulterated trust. It was that complete innocence, trust and belief in those thirteen-year-old pale blue eyes staring up at me that melted my heart.

How could someone do what they did to this kid, this bright young child?

This girl had already been through enough.

And from people she had put her trust in.

I would not let her down.

"I promise, Bridge. I won't leave your side until you're safely back with your mother."

She snuggled herself tighter against me. Her anxiety was replaced by waves of safety, security, trust, and comfort. "Thank you, Michael." She said it in a voice so low, so weak, so exhausted, that a normal human ear would not have been able to detect it.

But I heard it. And I felt the confusion, fear, and angst that filled this poor child's being.

Is this how a parent felt when they watched a child hurting? It was almost unbearable. How did parents handle it?

The train began to slow again.

The male voice over the PA system announced. "Hartford will be our next stop. We are arriving in Hartford."

I wondered how I might try to accomplish getting her safely back to her mother...when I would be turning into a wolf well before we made it to our destination in Stowe.

4:32 PM

I WOKE WITH a start.

Bridget was still sleeping in the chair across from me.

Outside, the sound of someone trying the door. That was what had woken me. It was Bruce. Again. I knew him by his odors and his still-angry emotion, by that familiar heartbeat. He wasn't giving up. He knew she was on this train and hiding, and he was determined to find her. But I had sealed the curtain with the Velcro strip, and he couldn't see in at all.

I could hear him trying other doors along the way. A few doors down, one of them opened. I heard him shuffle inside and look around. More anger flared when he didn't find who he was looking for. Then he moved on.

He had repeated that same relentless searching both times. The exact same pattern. Try every door; search through the ones that were open, and move on.

Conflict raced through me. Just like it had the previous time he'd been outside the door.

I wanted to stand up, throw open the door and wring his neck. I wanted to hurt him for hurting Bridget.

But my priority was keeping Bridget safe and hidden from him. And getting her to her mother.

Bruce finished his search through the last empty compartment, then exited the car.

Earlier, I hadn't even realized I had nodded off until I woke up. Again, I wondered at the gentle and rhythmic underlying pulse of the train and the effect it could have on a person. Across from me, Bridget was still sleeping in the seat. Bruce hadn't disturbed her at all.

The poor dear had slept for almost two hours. Not long after she had relayed her story to me, the sense of relief had finally allowed her to succumb to exhaustion. Her facial features had softened. She looked a lot younger than she did when she was awake.

I wondered where these overwhelming paternal instincts were coming from. I'd never really wanted kids. But I knew that male wolves were paternal. After I'd figured out what had happened to me, I read everything I could to understand wolves. Wolf blood ran through my veins, providing my human self with incredibly powerful wolf-life senses and strength. Was that same blood now infusing me with the same attentive and fiercely protective instincts?

"Hey," Bridget said, startling me out of my thoughts.

"Hey," I said. "Did you sleep okay?"

She sat up, yawned and stretched. "Like a baby. Wow, I was right out of it." She looked out the window. "Where are we?"

"We just left Massachusetts. We're in New Hampshire."

She gave off the essence of relief. She was that much closer to the safety and comfort of her mom. But then her emotions twisted, as she remembered the man she was hiding from.

"Any sign of Bruce?" she asked.

I wanted to tell her *no*, but I couldn't lie to her.

"He keeps searching; but he hasn't found us. He won't find us."

"But if he does..."

"He'll have to go through me first. I know I don't look like much, but I'm a lot tougher than I appear."

She smiled. "You're big. You're a thousand feet tall in my eyes. You're my favorite author. Besides Kelly Armstrong, that is."

I grinned and decided to use Bridget's love of fiction to distract her from the present moment. It was a subject I could talk about all day. "Oh yeah? I've met Kelly. She's a Canadian, like me. We met at a Comicon a few years ago. She is really sweet. A great writer; she writes some really dark stuff, but she's a genuinely really nice person. You'd really like her."

"I've been a fan of hers for a long time too. I loved her *Women of the Otherworld* series. Have you read them?"

"I've only read a few of her books. Just the first few in that series. I enjoyed the ones about Elena and the werewolf pack."

"Me, too. I love the whole series, but the first books about Elena are still my faves. Elena's one of my favorite characters. Have you seen the TV series based on Elena?"

"*Bitten?*" That was the name of the first book in that series. "No, I haven't seen it, but I hear it's pretty good."

"It's great! I really love it. It's in season two now. I like the books more, but the TV series allows me to get more of Elena."

She paused for a moment and looked back out the window.

"Funny, I actually just dreamt that Elena and I were racing through the woods together. We were searching for something, I'm not sure what, but we were running, side by side. She was in wolf form. I was me, but I was able to run fast, keep up with her. It was amazing."

I marvelled at the fact she had dreamed she was running alongside a wolf while, in reality, she had been racing across the countryside with a man who was also wolf. Was that some sort of preternatural instinct in her? Or just a strange coincidence?

It also made me worry again. I had to figure something out soon.

Or else, shortly after this train stopped in Waterbury, Bridget might just be *literally* running in a field beside a wolf.

6:28 PM

WE WERE PULLING out of White River Junction in Vermont when Bridget woke up the second time. This time as she had slept, I hadn't nodded off at all. I just sat there and watched her sleep, again marvelling at the beautiful innocence that overcame her features once she drifted off.

While she was asleep, my stomach began to growl and rumble. I needed to eat. Unsurprisingly, I was a voracious eater during this time of the month. Sure, I'd had a hearty "trucker's special" style breakfast before heading to Penn Station. But I was ready to eat again. I was pretty certain Bridget must also be starving.

I wanted to get up and go get us something to eat from the dining car. But these doors didn't lock from the outside, only the inside. Bruce had come back two more times. The desperation in him kept growing the longer he stalked back and forth through the car, continually searching, finding nothing.

"Hey," Bridget said, shortly after opening her eyes. "Where are we now?"

"We're in Vermont. It's almost six thirty. We just left White River Junction. Three stops and we'll be in Waterbury."

Waterbury. The final stop before she needed to head north to Stowe. Her train was scheduled to arrive at ten to eight. Less than half an hour before the sun went down.

She smiled at me. It was a genuine smile, one of wonder and friendship and trust.

"I still can't believe I'm hanging out with Michael freakin' Andrews," she whispered. "The brilliantly talented author, and now my hero."

"And I can't believe I'm hanging out with Bridget freakin' Wells." I replied. "Seriously. You're the most well-read person I've ever met. When did you become such a voracious reader?"

"My whole life. Mom tells me when I was really young, I started to read words aloud along with her as she read to me. She'd thought I just memorized words from the page, because it was a book she'd read to me countless times. But then she tried a new book, and when I started reading it along with her, she said she knew.

"I read everything I could get my hands on. I couldn't get enough. I started reading young-adult novels by the time I was six, and since about age eight I have been reading regular novels. A lot of the classics. Dickens, Brontë, Tolkien. My favorite is *Howard's End* by E.M. Forster. But I like new books, too. Once I discover a writer I like, I try to read all their books, if I can get my hands on them at the library. I picked up one of your books when I was ten and have read all of them."

"You've likely read more books by age thirteen than the average adult will read in a lifetime."

She nodded, with a big grin on her face.

"That is so awesome!" I said. "Us writers need to know there are more voracious readers like you out there." I lifted a closed fist into the air between us.

She mimicked my gesture. We did a fist bump and she giggled.

Her giggle brought out her actual age, not the maturity level she displayed in her speech and interactions, not the maturity of her reading level, not the much older teenager she appeared to be on the surface. But a thirteen-year-old.

"You must be hungry, Bridge." I said.

She laughed. "I'm starving."

"I was waiting for you to wake up. These doors only lock from the inside. I'm going to get us something to eat. I need you to lock the door behind me."

Her nervousness was palpable in the air suddenly. "All right," she said.

"It'll be okay," I said in a reassuring voice. "He's not out there right now. Lock the door behind me and make sure the curtains are tightly sealed. I won't be long. When I come back I'll use a code word to let you know it's me."

She smiled at the playfulness of that.

"I could use something like *Forester*. The author of your favorite novel."

"No," she said. "Let's use *Bronte*. Because I also love the books by both the Brontë sisters and that's also the name of the main character in your books."

I grinned. "*Bronte* it is."

As I slipped out of the car, Bridget pushed the door closed behind me. I could hear Bridget slide the lock latch closed, as well as the rapid beat of her heart and increased rate of breathing.

I made my way out of the sleeper car and back through the coach car I had been sitting in originally. My backpack was sitting on the seat where I'd left it, completely unmolested. I grabbed the backpack and found my way through the other cars and to the dining car. I could detect Bruce's smell throughout each car, but I didn't actually see him anywhere along my route. Which meant he must be in one of the other sleeper cars, toward the front of the train.

I settled into the queue of people lined up at the service bar in the dining car. The overhead PA announced that we would be arriving in Randolph Station.

When the train pulled to a stop at the station, I was still in line, bemused at the reactions of the people ahead of me: the mixed emotions and feelings of hunger, anger over the wait and, in the case of an impeccably dressed older lady who looked like she should be having high tea with the Queen of England rather than on a dining car on an Amtrak train, a continually ongoing case of serial flatulence. Her farts were silent to normal ears, but the ungodly smell was detectable to everyone. Most of the others in line threw annoyed glances at a nearby biker dude. I was amused at how they assumed he was the perpetrator of the gaseous infestation, and not the sweet old lady.

I finally got my food as the PA announced that the train was about to leave the station, and I started walking back through the diner and lounge cars as the train began to slowly move forward.

As I entered the first coach car, I smelled the distinct scent of Bridget's fear.

It wasn't a lingering scent from before, but a fresh, more powerful one.

And, oddly, it wasn't coming from the cars ahead of me.

I was picking it up off the air vent, tinged with a burst of fresh air.

Bridget was outside!

I looked out the window to my right and spotted her rushing down a street beside the train station.

With Bruce right behind her.

The train was picking up speed. They disappeared behind a warehouse-sized building.

I rushed back to where the coach car connected with the lounge car. The exit door was unlocked. Dirt and gravel sped past as we continued to accelerate out of the station.

I leapt out, clearing the gravel. My feet hit the hard-packed dirt, and the forward momentum pitched me forward. I tucked and rolled, losing my backpack and the sandwiches in the process.

The train rushed past.

I came out of my tumble and raised myself to my feet.

I ran along the trail of Bridget's scent, picking up where Bruce's odor intersected with hers. He was closer, gaining on her.

I followed their scents to the open doorway of a rickety, three-story wooden structure that looked like some sort of mill.

Just as I was stepping into the shadowy interior of the warehouse building, wood cracked as it connected with flesh and bone. The sound echoed through the mostly empty space, along with a yelp of surprise and pain from Bruce.

About twenty feet ahead of me, at the door of an inner room, Bridget had ambushed him with an old two-by-four.

He was still standing. A long slash on the left side of his head was just starting to bleed.

The board was old and weathered. It had done some damage, but not enough.

I ran toward them.

Bruce grabbed her wrist with one hand and easily twisted her off balance. She squealed in pain as she flopped to the floor on her side.

"You stupid bitch. That's twice you've hit me," he yelled, dabbing at the blood streaming down the side of his face. "I wanted to talk to you about what happened. Explain. But now I'm going to fuck you so hard you won't be able to walk! Then I'm going to shut you up for good."

"No!" Bridget said, striking at him with her free hand. "Let me go!"

A split second before I reached Bruce, he turned his head to look.

I slammed into the side of his chest with my right elbow. He was a solid guy. Even through that quick hit, I could feel the tight and thick muscles on his chest. But the blow was hard enough to knock him off his feet and send him flying against the old wooden wall. Weathered, like the board Bridget had found, the wall cracked and buckled.

"You're not touching her again!" I growled.

He shook his head and started to pick himself up.

I bent down and put out my hand to Bridget. "You okay?" I helped her to her feet.

Bruce was upright now. "This is none of your fucking business. I'm gonna fuck you up."

The man's muscles and fighting stance made me pause.

As I've said, I'm not a fighter. Never have been. Prior to me coming into my supernatural powers, I'm pretty sure I'd have been a quick knockout.

Bruce rushed at me and sent a right hook for my chin. His anger made him sloppy. I dodged away from it, my right arm pounding into his ribs. Beneath the layer of tight muscle on his ribs, I felt and heard them crack. I realized I hadn't tried to pull my punch, as I always did since I'd been turned. My own anger had gotten the better of me.

"Fuck!" Bruce shuffled a few steps away.

"Language!" I said to him. "There's a young person in the room."

I had always wondered, why Spider-Man was such a wise-cracker. Since my change, I'd learned that, at least for me, it was a way to relieve the tension of conflict. In a tense fight situation, it just spouted out of me.

Plus the cheeky ribbing I'd just given him—get it, ribbing?—angered him more.

I could tell Bruce was tensing for a surprise attack just before he ducked down and lunged at me. But I didn't have enough time to get out of the way of the full body tackle.

He hit me hard enough to throw me off balance and we both stumbled to the floor. As we landed, he rained quick, fast blows with his right hand to my own ribs.

With no give between his fists and the concrete floor, I felt one of my own ribs crack.

"Copy-cat!" I blurted as the wind was knocked out of me. "Try one of your own moves."

He raised his left arm up and elbowed me hard in the mouth. I could immediately taste the blood. Then his closed right fist hit the right side of my face.

"That's better," I quipped, hoping my voice could be heard through the sudden ringing in my head. "Good for you. You get to advance to the next level."

The truth was, I was hurting. But I didn't want him to know that.

Bruce slammed his elbow into my nose and sent another punch to the side of my head.

Then I heard another crack.

Bridget stood over him with a broken two-by-four in her hand, the other end bouncing away across the floor. It hadn't hurt him but provided a much-needed distraction. I'm not a fan of being pummelled.

I bucked, bringing my knees up and lifting him into the air to launch him over my head. He hit the floor with his right shoulder as he rolled onto his back.

"Thanks, Bridge," I said as I shifted around to my feet.

Bruce was in the process of getting up, still in a crouched position as I rushed him. This time my right elbow connected with the soft spot between his left shoulder and neck. He crumpled down to his knees.

With my right hand, I grabbed him near the back of his neck and lifted him off his feet. Then I shoved my left hand into his face and stepped forward, pushing him back against the wooden wall with the back of his head leading the way.

The wood splintered and cracked.

I let him drop. He managed to stay on his feet.

I punched him in the ribs again, this time with my left hand. I didn't pull the punch. There was a much more audible cracking this time. He buckled forward and let out a yelp. I slapped his face hard with an open right hand, snapping his head to the left, then followed that with a backhand that caught him dead center and broke his nose.

I paused, smelling that the fight was out of him. He was in full defensive mode, trying to back away. He backed into the wall and put one hand out to keep his balance, barely able to stay on his feet.

As I was trying to figure out what to do next, Bridget stepped up from my left, got right in front of him and thrust her right foot up, her shin catching him squarely between the legs.

He crumpled to the floor, unconscious.

"Nice legwork, kiddo," I smiled at her.

She smiled back at me. "Nice work yourself." Her scent became infused with worry. "Oh no, your nose is bleeding. So is your lip."

"I'm okay." I said. "I'll be okay." I cradled my left side. "My ribs feel a lot worse than my face looks." Blood from my nose and lip had leaked onto the front of the gray t-shirt I was wearing. I grabbed the material and used it to dab at my lip and nose.

"We've got to take care of him," I said.

"Let's call the police!" she said.

"No," I said, thinking about the time. It was going to be sundown soon. "Not yet. Not right now. This might sound strange, but I can't be involved with that."

"Oh," she said. "You're a celebrity. You don't want the tabloids to know. That makes sense."

Best to let her believe that. "Thanks for understanding." I said. "But we also need to make sure he can't follow you. Not that I think he'll have it in him to do much more than go crawl somewhere and lick his wounds."

I explained that if we took his clothes, tossed his wallet into a ditch somewhere a few blocks away, it would limit his ability to follow any longer. What I didn't tell her was that, since Bruce was a bit larger than me, his clothes would at least come in handy for me to wear in the morning—as soon as I figured out the logistics of how that was going to work, now that I had a travelling companion.

We left Bruce completely naked. I suppose we could have left him in his underwear, because I certainly hadn't planned on wearing them. But I wanted to leave him completely naked and vulnerable. I had certainly woken up enough times in that state. I was an old pro at it. But the experience would likely be a new one for him. Catching Bridget would be the furthest thing from his mind.

I wrapped his t-shirt around his jeans in a tightly wadded ball. I also wrapped his boxers around his wallet. One bundle to keep for later; the other to dispose of. "Okay," I said. "We need to get out of here."

"There's blood on your shirt," Bridget said. "People will notice."

The front of my t-shirt was most certainly a mess. The right side of my chest was a dark-red Rorschach blob.

"We'll have to try to take a way where nobody sees us," I said.

"Why don't you just wear his shirt?"

"I have another idea for how to use his shirt," I said. "I'll explain later. Let's get going."

"Why don't you just wear his t-shirt over top of yours for now?"

Smart kid. I grinned at her. "Good idea." I unwrapped Bruce's t-shirt from the bundle and pulled it over my head.

"Okay," I said. "Let's move. We have to get as much space as we can between us and Bruce, as quickly as possible."

We made our way out of the old wooden warehouse. Nobody was on the narrow side-street on the other side of the train tracks; nobody would see us leaving the warehouse and thus connect us to the naked, unconscious man inside.

"This way," I said.

We walked down the back street to where it hooked around to the left, then connected with a larger street, still running parallel to the tracks. The stop sign at that inter-section told us it was Weston Street. We turned right onto Weston.

"How did you know I'd gotten off the train?" Bridget asked. "How did you find me?"

"I saw you running. I guessed that you might try to hide in that empty warehouse."

She looked at me funny; her scent told me she knew I wasn't being entirely truthful.

"How did Bruce find you?" I asked. "Did he get in the cabin? How did you get away from him? Did you hit him?"

"Oh," she said, and her scent took on an air of embar-rassment. "I was stupid." She shuffled forward a few steps, absently kicking at a stone on the path in front of us.

"It's okay," I said. "You don't need to tell me. It doesn't matter what happened. All that matters is you're all right. And you're not stupid, Bridge."

"No," she said after a pause and more pebble kicking. "I *was* stupid. I had to pee. The toilet in the cabin we were in didn't work. I *really* had to pee. The train had stopped to let people off. I peeked out the curtains and didn't see anyone in the hall. I figured I'd try one of the other cabins and use the toilet there. But the minute I stepped into the hall, Bruce called to me.

"He was at the corner at the end of the car. So I ran in the opposite direction. I didn't know how far down the diner car was. When I got to the car with all the regular seats, the door was open. I felt trapped. I went out the door and the second I stepped off the train I ran."

"See," I said. "You weren't stupid. You knew the best option to get away. You were right. Being on the train was a dead end."

"Maybe," she said. "But at least being on the train meant I was going to get to my Mom's. Now I don't even have that."

"We'll find a way."

We were both quiet on the rest of our walk up that long street. I could tell Bridget was worried, wondering about how we were going to get to her mom's. Me, I was trying to figure out a plan to keep her safe. I didn't want to get tickets for the next train out of Randolph. We needed to be as far away from Bruce as possible, just to be safe.

I couldn't be around Bridget overnight anyway. I had to get her somewhere safe so she could continue her journey to her mother without me. I didn't want to leave her alone, but it wasn't like I had much choice. In less than an hour, I would be turning into a wolf.

I didn't know how to tell her I'd be leaving her after promising I wouldn't.

It took about ten minutes for us to make it to the end of Weston Street, where Weston and the tracks again met.

The sound of running water was not far ahead.

"Let's follow the tracks from here," I said. "Put a little more distance between us and Bruce."

"Sure," she said. "But give me a minute. I can't take the sound of running water. Remember the reason I left the train car in the first place."

She rushed off the side of the trail into a set of the bushes. I was confused.

"Look the other way," she called out, even though she was barely hidden behind the foliage.

"Where are you…?"

"Michael," she said. "Turn around. I have to pee."

"Whoops, sorry." I laughed, turning around.

I tried to block out the sounds as I stood there, completely embarrassed for both of us, while waiting for her to finish. For a man with extra heightened senses and abilities, I sometimes really didn't pick up on the subtle things.

In a hundred yards, the tracks crossed a brook. I stopped on the bridge and opened Bruce's wallet, removing the cash and handing it to Bridget. "You might as well hang on to this." I wrapped Bruce's underwear around the wallet again and tossed it high into the air over the water.

The underwear unfurled and landed on a branch hanging over the water. The wallet itself came down another twenty feet or so past that, and landed with a satisfying splash in the brook.

"There," I said. "I don't think he'll find that any time soon."

"Anytime, ever," Bridget giggled.

We kept walking in that same direction along the tracks, trees on both sides. We continued in our silence. The quiet, the trees on both sides of us, were conducive to me coming up with a plan.

After another fifteen minutes or so, we got to a longer bridge, this one crossing a larger body of water. I figured it must be close to eight o'clock. I had maybe fifteen minutes before I turned into my canine form.

From the sounds and smells, to our left was a large ex-
panse of forest. Up ahead there were more people, some
roads, traffic, the scent of wood-burning stoves and
campfires. Likely another small subdivision of homes,
maybe even a campground.

I figured that stashing Bruce's t-shirt and jeans (as well
as my own jeans) under the tracks might work. This
could be a good spot for me to change. I just had to send
Bridget on up ahead.

"Did you ever see the movie *Stand By Me*?" I said, as
we stood in front of the bridge.

"No," she said. "But I read the novella by Stephen
King that it was based on."

"Of course you did," I laughed.

"You're thinking of the bridge scene," she said.

"Yeah. Every time I see a set of train tracks over a river,
I think of that."

"Are you worried about a train coming?" she asked.

"No," I said. "I can tell there isn't one coming."

"How?"

"I don't hear anything," I said. And I reached down to
feel the tracks. "And you can actually feel the vibrations
if there's one not that far away."

"Okay, I don't get it, Michael." Her scent was filled
with confusion. "What does this have to do with that Stephen King book?"

"Listen, Bridget," I said, reaching into my pocket for
my small wad of cash.

"Bridge," she said. "My friends call me Bridge."

"Bridge. You're the same age as the kids in that movie.
And you're much smarter than they were. I need you to

keep going along these tracks until you find a house where you can call the police. I can't go any further with you. I really wish I could. But it's something I can't really explain."

"What?" she said, her tone and scent completely incredulous. "Why aren't you coming?"

"I...I don't know how to explain. Just trust me. Look, it's going to be dark soon. You should get going. There are some houses up ahead. You can get help." I pulled out my cash and handed it to her. "Here. You might need this. Just in case."

"No!" she said.

"Bridget, I can't go on. I want to help you get to your mother. But I can't go any further. I can't be seen after dark. I need to be alone."

"What?" she said. "Do you turn into a pumpkin at midnight or something?"

"Please," I said. "I need to know you'll be safe. Go on ahead. Find the first house. It's not that far ahead. Tell them what happened. You'll be okay."

"How do you *know* that?" she asked.

"Just go, Please."

"No! We're in this together. I need to get to my mom. You said you needed to visit a sick friend. And besides, you promised me. So I'm not going anywhere without you."

"Please," I said. "Bridge, there isn't much time."

"Time for what? Michael, we are friends. You helped me. I can help you. Just let me know and we can get through this."

She was thirteen going on thirty in terms of her emotional intelligence and maturity. A bright and brave kid. And an open-minded one. And I knew, because I could smell it on her, that was not going anywhere, no matter what I said, no matter what I did to try to convince her.

For a moment I considered running, sprinting really fast, losing her in the woods. But if she followed me, and she would, she might get lost. At least here, she was on the tracks. There was a clear direction. She knew there were some houses up ahead.

I needed to convince her it was better for her to go on without me

But after what we'd already been through, what could I say, in fifteen minutes or less, to make her leave without me? Maybe, instead, in the time I had, I could explain it to her.

She had already been lied to, been betrayed; the thought of being anything but honest with her was at the forefront of my mind. Any other options I might have been considering started to skitter away.

I at least owed it to her to try.

I sighed.

"Okay," I said to her. "I'll explain. But it's not going to be easy to tell you."

"Do you think," she said, "that it was easy for me to tell you about what Bruce did to me, and what he tried to do to me?"

"No, you're right. You trusted me. So it's time I returned the favor and trusted you. I'm about to share a secret I haven't ever told anyone else before. In fact, only one other person knows, and I never even told her. She figured it out on her own."

A deep and rich empathy flowed from Bridge as she reached out and took my hand. "Please tell me."

I shouldn't have been surprised. This was in keeping with the rest of her incredible maturity; but it was also startling that this girl whose childhood had been snatched from her less than twenty-four hours ago was suddenly comforting an adult.

Perhaps it's easier to comfort another person than to wallow in one's own predicament.

But nonetheless I was impressed.

"You remember that dream you had about running in the field with Elena the werewolf from Kelly Armstrong's novels?"

"Yeah."

"Well, what I'm going to tell you, it's like…that."

"No way," she said, and I could tell from her scent that she had already pieced enough of it together, slowly, in her head, to believe me. "*Noooooo waaaaaaaay!*"

Saturday August 1, 2015

6:12 AM

I WOKE UP curled up in a ball, or maybe more like a fetal position. Normally, when I woke up, it was more of an awakening of my consciousness. Like I had just recently resumed human form from the wolf persona. But this was a waking from sleep; as if I had actually morphed into human form while asleep as a wolf. It wasn't sunrise, but shortly after. I just know these things. Like when you just know that you can't trust a particular fart.

I was naked, lying on a wooden floor inside some sort of structure. I could feel something draped over me. It was a t-shirt, laid overtop of me like a blanket. Someone was pressed up against my back, and I could feel and hear the rhythmic sleep-breathing of the person nestled tight up against me, as if we had been snuggling while we slept.

The person was female. But it wasn't Gail.

I knew her, though. The scent seemed oddly familiar.

The cloth on top of me offered a familiar scent, and I immediately recognized the scent on it as Bruce, the guy I had nicknamed Cornflake when I'd first spotted him on the train.

Then it came to me all at once. Bruce. *Bridget.*

I wiggled my naked body away from her, feeling like some sort of perverted old man. I tried to remind myself that she had been snuggling with a wolf, not all that different than curling up to sleep with a dog. Thank goodness she was still asleep.

As I looked at her peaceful, sleeping form, I wanted nothing more than to protect her from the darkness of the world, help bring her the same sense of peace she experienced in sleep, when she woke.

I was reminded of my promise to get her to her mother.

Looking around, I deduced we were in some sort of small shed. The earthy scent of shovels and other yard tools clued me in to that as much as the visual overview. There was a single, small window beside the door to the shed. Scuttling further away from Bridget, I kept myself covered with Bruce's t-shirt. No sense freaking her out if she woke up. I spotted a pile of clothes to my right. My jeans, Bruce's jeans. My t-shirt. Bruce's t-shirt. Socks. My running shoes. No underwear. I figured I must have had those on when I'd changed the night before.

Damn, I hate piecing together missing time.

I often had very little memory of the last five to ten minutes before turning into wolf form. I didn't know exactly what Bridget and I had spoken about or what had happened. I knew what I had planned on telling her. But all I could remember was that I had started to tell her and that she seemed to believe me even before I could get to the details.

Then my memory went blank.

Probing the fleeting memories of the past ten hours, I was able to come up with a few images of walking alongside a young human female beside a set of train tracks.

Of course, my wolf mind didn't know they were train tracks, just that they seemed to be some sort of unnatural, human-built structure. But, looking back at that wolf memory, I knew what they were.

Another memory. It was of a vehicle passing by on a nearby road. The human female was hunkered down beside me, whispering that it was okay. I remember being frightened of the bright light and the roaring sound of the engine as the vehicle passed us.

There were two other memories, mostly auditory. The first one was the human female saying, "It feels weird calling you Michael when you're in this form. How about Mikey? That seems like a much more fitting name for you. Mikey." The second one was the same voice saying, "Okay, Mikey, you need to settle down. It's time to get some sleep." That memory came with the feeling of being snuggled into a tight hug.

I pulled my jeans on, then Bruce's t-shirt. I made a note at how forward-thinking Bridget had been. She must have carried my clothes with her last night while I was in wolf form.

Like I said, a bright kid.

I got to my feet and looked out the window.

There was a dirt laneway and a large, barn-shaped structure on the left, and, past that, on the right, a white house with red shutters. I could smell at least five distinct human scents coming from the general direction of the house.

To the right, down the laneway, a hand-painted sign with some sort of flower in the middle and a cursive script read *Johnnycake Flats Bed & Breakfast*.

I had to assume we were still in Vermont. Perhaps a bit north from Randolph. I had planned on telling Bridget to just keep following the train tracks north; it was the best way to get us where we needed to be. Eventually. But how far north had we made it? How close were we to Waterbury, which was the Vermonter's last stop?

Bridget was still sleeping peacefully. I marvelled at how she had rolled with the punches, accepted what I was, and continued on the quest to see her mother. She had obviously put faith in me as her canine companion. We must have walked for miles in the dead of night.

Was I ever this bright, this brave, this flexible, when I was thirteen?

I sincerely doubted it.

Her heartbeat and breathing started to change as she moved out of a deep sleep and into a lighter mode. She was beginning to wake. I stood and watched her for a minute until her eyelids fluttered open.

A huge smile beamed across her face as she lifted her head. "You're back!"

"I am. Thanks for taking care of me when I was in wolf form, Bridge."

"Are you kidding? Thanks for taking care of me. I was terrified out there. It was pitch black in some spots. Sure, there were some houses along the way, some streetlights and traffic on a nearby road here and there. The main highway and the train tracks kept splitting off from one another. But most of the time, the only light we had was the full moon."

"That full moon can be both a blessing and a curse."

She laughed. "I imagined we were Mowgli and the wolf-pack leader Akela on a midnight romp through the jungle." Of course she was familiar with *The Jungle Book*.

"Did you sleep okay?" I asked.

"Yeah, I think so."

"Was it scary? Watching me turn into a wolf?"

She said, "I watched this childbirth video last year in health class. It was both scary and disgusting. But that video had *nothing* on watching what happened to you. I thought you were dying. I didn't know what to do. And then you were standing there on all fours, looking at me, your tongue hanging out. You seemed to recognize me. It was freaky, but not scary. Um…I called you Mikey. You reacted to that."

"Do you know how far we went?"

"I don't know. All I know is that I was tired. I tried this shed door. It wasn't locked." She got up and came over the window and looked out. "Nice place," she said. "Where are we?"

"It's a bed and breakfast."

She rubbed her stomach and I could actually hear its low rumble. "Oh yeah, I could use some breakfast."

8:28 AM

"SINCERELY, IT'S TRULY my pleasure," Jim said. "I only wish I could take you the whole way there."

Jim was driving. Bridget and I cozied up beside him on the bench seat of his pickup truck, me on the far right and Bridget nestled between us. Tight fit, but not uncomfortable. Jim drove with both hands on the steering wheel, as conscientious a driver as he was a host of the bed and breakfast he and his wife Debra owned and ran, Johnnycake Flats. Their passion for hospitality, conversation, and just plain neighborly love was unfounded.

Bridget and I had walked from the shed and up the main building at Johnnycake Flats. We gave them the story that I was Bridget's uncle and we were on our way to visit my sister-in-law, her mother, in Stowe, when our car broke down several miles down the highway in the middle of the night. We explained that there was nothing we could do to fix the car, so we'd spent the night walking and hitch-hiking, hoping to get somewhere we could call Bridget's mother. We made up an excuse that we didn't own cellular devices, preferring old-fashioned conversation and human connections, and asked if we could use their phone to call Bridget's mother.

Jim and Debra immediately welcomed us in. Their scent didn't reveal a drop of mistrust or disbelief in either of them, although they thought it was strange about the cell phones. They were both very trusting souls. And generous, too. No sooner had they showed Bridget where the phone was, that they were offering us coffee and suggesting that we sit down to eat because we must be exhausted from the walking.

Bridget called her mother, but it went straight to her mobile phone's voice mail. She ended up leaving a message, telling her that she was on her way and would be there later that day. She didn't leave any specifics.

We had the most amazing farm-to-table breakfast I think I have ever had in my life. Debra kept piling more onto our plates in a seemingly never-ending buffet. When the meal was finished, Bridget tried calling her mother again and, for a second time, got her answering machine. Jim insisted on driving us into town. He actually said that if he hadn't already promised to do a favor for a friend at nine a.m., he would have been delighted to drive us all the way to Stowe. Even their dog, a border collie named Toby, was friendly and personable. He stayed right at my feet the entire time we were sitting at the dinner table, and I could smell off him the special kinship he'd felt toward me. Most animals could sense the canine elements running through me, and sometimes made strange with me. But not Toby. We were immediate pals. It was as if he were cut from the very same "friendliness" cloth as Jim and Debra.

I hated lying to such a sweet and trusting couple. But what was I supposed to tell them? *So here's the deal, Jim. I'm a werewolf, originally from Canada, but now living in Manhattan. I'm trying to help this thirteen-year-old, who I just met and who escaped nearly being raped, to get to her mother's place.* I didn't think that would fly. Better for this delightful couple to think I was Bridget's uncle and that she was much older than she appeared to be. Better for them to not have any questions.

As Jim pulled into the bus station in Montpelier, he apologized—again—for not being able to take us the whole way there. I assured him that he was a huge lifesaver and that we appreciated everything he and his wife had done for us. We shook hands and thanked him again, and he wished us good luck before his pickup truck pulled back onto the street.

As Jim's truck pulled away, Toby stared back at us with his mouth partially open in what appeared to be a huge grin.

Naturally.

8:58 AM

THE BUS WE were on between Montpelier and Waterbury wasn't much larger than an extended-length van. There were six rows of seats. Bridget and I were in the fourth seat from the front. Half a dozen other passengers were on this route, which left Montpelier at 8:42 a.m. and was to arrive in Waterbury about half an hour later. We had opted not to take the Greyhound, which wouldn't have left for several hours. A youngster a couple of seats ahead sang a song from a popular children's television program.

The situation reminded me of a scene from one of my favorite movies. Bridget and I were like John Candy and Steve Martin in *Planes, Trains, and Automobiles*, trying desperately to make our way from New York to Chicago in time for Thanksgiving, failing, and having to resort to multiple transportation options.

I watched her as she started out the window.

"Oh," she blurted, turning from the window. "I never told you what I said to my mom when I left her that message. I mentioned that I didn't have my phone on me and that I was on my way. That I was with a friend, I was safe. And I would explain everything once I got there."

"Uh, yeah," I said. "I know. I could hear you."

She giggled. Then she whispered. "I keep forgetting you have enhanced senses. That must be so strange."

"It was at first," I said, also in a low voice. "But I've gotten used to it. I do have to sometimes consciously block things out, but I can easily fine-tune and hone in on a specific sound. Like, right now I can focus in on just the beating of your heart and I'm blocking out the other sounds—the other folks talking, the music coming from the earbuds of someone at the front of the bus. The sound of the engine. The gum-smacking of the driver."

"So with all the smells you can smell," Bridget said. "You must be able to read people. Like you're a human lie detector."

"It is handy," I agreed.

"So you're really good at reading and understanding people, right?"

"Pretty much."

"Then how did you lose the woman you love so much? How did Gail break up with you?"

I paused, stunned. "How did you know about Gail?"

"You told me about her last night before your change. You were explaining that only one other person knew, and that was the friend you were going to see who had a sick uncle. I asked a few things about who she was, and you shared that the two of you had once dated, but that she broke it off years ago and you were now good friends."

I chuckled. "You don't need my special senses to read me like a book."

"So are you going to tell her? Are you going to tell Gail how much you still love her?"

"No," I said. "I'm going there to be the friend that she needs. Just a friend."

Bridget was silent for about a minute before she spoke up again. "Why didn't you call Gail when we were back at the bus station?"

"Yeah," I could feel my face turning red. "Here's the thing. Because I don't actually remember her phone number. It's programmed into my phone."

Bridget laughed. "Too bad you weren't bitten by a radioactive elephant."

"What?"

"You have all these extra wolf powers and abilities, right?"

"Uh-huh."

"But an elephant. That would bring you super memory."

"Funny," I kept a straight face. "That, and the fact I'd always have a trunk to pack a change of clothes in."

She rolled her eyes. "That's bad. That's stupid dad-joke material."

Then she fell silent. I think saying that made her think about her father. I could smell the anxiety and anger and confusion boiling within her emotions.

I reached over and took hold of her hand, squeezing it gently.

She squeezed back, letting me know she was okay.

We held hands for the rest of the bus ride without saying anything else to one another. In some ways, Bridget reminded me of Gail. Gail was also quite adept at reading people, at understanding and accepting them. And, like Bridget, Gail's younger years hadn't been all that easy. But she had managed to make her way through it and become a remarkable woman that I respected and admired so much.

While Bridget was going through a tough time now — her parents' separation, Bruce's attempt to molest her, the startling realization of some of the darkness of the world — she would likely make it through this and become even stronger. Just like Gail.

As the bus was pulling into our stop, right beside the train station, I could detect the scent of a woman filled with an extreme amount of anxiety. Her scent carried a familiarity to it. Bridget's mother.

I squeezed Bridget's hand. "Good news," I said. "Your mother's here."

Bridget's heart rate sped up. "Really?"

"Yup."

She turned and smiled at me. "Thank you, Michael."

"I couldn't have made it here without your help. Thank you, Bridge. But, as we discussed, it's best to leave me out of this. I was just a stranger whose name you never learned. Much easier for me not to have to explain. Go, be with your mother."

"But my Mom can drive you to Burlington. To Gail."

"I'll be fine," I said. "You take care of *you*. I'm almost there. I'll be there soon enough. If I have to stop to answer questions, it'll keep me from getting to Gail in Burlington.

I'd prefer to just remain anonymous in this story. A friendly stranger. It'll be easier."

She let go of my hand, turned in the seat and gave me a giant hug. "Thank you. For everything. You've been like a big brother to me." In my ear, she whispered, "You know I won't tell anyone about your secret. It's one hundred percent safe with me."

"I never doubted that for a second, Bridge," I whispered back.

As the bus finished parking and stopped, Bridget moved back from the hug. "Can I call you? Can I stay in touch?"

"Of course," I said. "I'll need to know you're okay."

"What's your number? How do I contact you?"

"I don't even know my own cell number. I never call it. But I live at The Algonquin Hotel in Manhattan."

She slugged me in the arm. "I'll figure it out."

"Go," I said. "Your mom smells like a giant ball of nerves. She'll be over the moon to see that you're safe."

She smiled as she got out of the seat.

"I hope Gail's uncle is going to be okay," she said. "You should talk to Gail about how you feel about her."

I just offered a tight-lipped grin.

"Off you go, kiddo," I said.

She moved off the bus and I heard her mother squeal in delight upon seeing her. The scent of love, of concern, of overwhelming relief was almost overpowering as I could hear her mother embracing Bridget in a beautiful, motherly hug.

I focused on trying to block out their conversation, not wanting to eavesdrop. I waited until everyone else on the bus got off before I got up. I wanted to give Bridge and her mother time to move on and away. The bus driver told me the best way to get to Burlington was to take the 86 route, which was the fastest, or the Greyhound or the Red Line, if I preferred. "You've got plenty of options," he said, smiling at me. "But they'll all get you where you need to be."

Where I needed to be.

I needed to be with Gail. And, thanks to the support, friendship, and wisdom of my new friend Bridget, I would arrive there a much wiser person. Maybe this time I wouldn't screw it up. Maybe I would follow Bridge's sage advice. She had, after all, pulled my skin out of the fire more than once in the past day and a half.

I climbed off the bus. Bridget and her mother were walking arm in arm several yards away.

Just as I looked, Bridget turned her head and offered me a wink and a smile.

"Thank you, Bronte." She whispered in a voice so quiet not even her mother could hear it.

But she knew I could.

Thank you, I mouthed back. But she had already turned away.

Authors Notes & Sneak Peek

About Stowe Away

Stowe Away was originally published in **Amazing Monster Tales:** *Monster Road Trip*, Nov 2019.

A FUNNY THING happened to me on the way to writing the second book in my Canadian Werewolf series.

You might liken it to the funny things that happen to Michael Andrews when he wakes up with one intention of how he imagines his day might go, then ends up stumbling into all sorts of diversions, side tracks or mayhem, usually just because he recognizes a need and pauses to help someone out.

I knew that when I started writing more tales about the adventures of Michael Andrews, my Canadian Werewolf in New York, that I'd likely have him moving around a little bit, perhaps visiting different cities.

The very first inclination of that was when I started to pen the second book in the series, *Fear and Longing in Los Angeles*. I was, of course, having fun with the way that title was a bit of a nod to the title of the book (and tie-in movie) by Hunter S. Thompson, *Fear and Loathing in Las Vegas*. I liked that it was a play and twist on the familiar, in the same way that *A Canadian Werewolf in New York* was a play on the 1981 John Landis movie *An American Werewolf in London*.

Establishing that type of consistent pattern is important to me. Perhaps it's part of a larger branding exercise. With my non-fiction books about the paranormal, alliteration was the pattern I used. *Haunted Hamilton* was followed by *Spooky Sudbury*, *Tomes of Terror*, *Creepy Capital*, *Haunted Hospitals*, and *Macabre Montreal*. My very first short story collection *One Hand Screaming*, released in 2004, was followed by the eight-volume mini short story collection series I started in 2017 called *Nocturnal Screams*.

As of the writing of these notes, Michael's adventures in Los Angeles are still only about halfway done completion of the first draft. In the same way that the novel *A Canadian Werewolf in New York* (ACWWINY for short) had originally been started in 2006, but wasn't completed until 2014, and then published in 2016, I started off the novel, then put it aside while working on other projects. (If you've been patiently waiting for more and are upset with me about not having finished that next book yet, or are panicking that it might be a decade before that book is released, I'd like to assure you that (a) I beat myself up about my lack of forward momentum on that book at least once a week, and (b) working on this project, which I'll explain a bit more about in a bit, has motivated me to double down on my efforts to get that second book in the series out without the same overtly length delay that ACWWINY suffered).

The parallel patterns of the titles being a nod to books or movies, with a twist thrown into the title, is an intentional technique were I'm giving the reader something oddly familiar, and yet has an unexpected twist. It is perhaps in the same way that Michael lives in a world very much familiar to us, because it is our world, except that there's a bit of a twist. Werewolves and other supernatural creatures exist in this world. But not too many of them. Because I wanted it to be as normal a world as possible, just with that little twist to spice up, or flavor the world a little differently.

I didn't want the world to be one that was over-run by supernatural beings, but, instead, a normal one, with a little thrown in here and there for a bit of extra spice and flavor.

And that leads to a couple of the reasons I thought Michael should likely travel.

Sure, New York is a giant population, and thus, if there is one supernatural creature, like a werewolf – well technically, at least two, since we know Michael had been bitten by a werewolf before turning into one – there are bound to be others.

But I didn't want the New York I was writing about to be one that was filled with supernatural creatures. I didn't want it to be like the New York of the Marvel comic or cinematic universe. Don't get me wrong. I love that universe. I grew up on a diet of Spider-Man, Captain America, Daredevil, and other Marvel comics. But one thing that always bothered me about that world was just how crowded that large metropolis was with different superheroes, villains, and threats. Why, for example, was Spider-Man the only one around to save the day when some horrible creature was threatening the city? Why didn't the other dozen superheroes who lived in New York step up to save the day? And how could that be happening in the month of June, for example (the comic books were monthly), while, just down the street, Daredevil was fighting another similar larger threatening menace? They did have plenty of cross-over storylines, but considering the number of heroes and villains wandering around, I'd wonder why there weren't more accidental collisions between them all.

So, in order to maintain some semblance of normalcy to Michael's world, I had to have his supernatural abilities be that much more unique. My original intent, when I first sat down to create his character, was an attempt to explore what it might be like to try to live a normal life with supernatural abilities and a bit of a predilection for assuming responsibility. Most of the "bad guys" he would encounter, would, and should be normal humans.

In fact, the other wolf that Michael encounters in *A Canadian Werewolf in New York* isn't even a local resident living in New York. He is a musician on tour.

And so, while New York is a big city, with millions of people, and also plenty of visitors, I didn't want to fall into what I call "The *Murder, She Wrote* Conceit." *Murder She Wrote* was an extremely successful television series from 1984 to 1996 starring Angela Lansbury as Jessica Fletcher, a mystery writer and amateur detective. The show was set in Cabot Cove, a small coastal town in

Maine. To have that many murders happen in such a small community in a single decade, all of them requiring the meddling of an amateur detective to solve, was not only extremely unlikely, it was a little outrageous. An August 2012 article in *The Telegraph* by Anita Singh entitled "Murder She Wrote location named as murder capital of the world" stated than an estimated two percent of the town's population (approximately 3,500) made it's murder rate 60% higher than Honduras, the real-life murder capital of the world (where there is a violent death every 74 minutes).

Those were the reasons I needed to have Michael travel at least a little bit in his ongoing adventures.

But I never imagined him getting onto a train.

Nor that he would end up returning to a shorter length format, where his character was originally born.

And for these two things, I blame (or, more aptly, praise and thank) Jamie Ferguson and Deanna Knippling, the editors of the *Amazing Monster Tales* series of anthologies. I had provided a reprint story to them for the first volume in that series, and then, in January 2019, they announced they would be reading for a few future themed issues. One of them was going to be called *Monster Road Trip*.

I wondered if that might be the perfect excuse to revisit Michael on his uncompleted Los Angeles adventure. But that would be an 80,000-word novel. I spent some time pondering how I could adapt my plans for that into something shorter, but then abandoned that idea.

A Canadian Werewolf in New York takes place in the summer of 2014. *Fear and Longing in Los Angeles* is set in 2017. I did that because I wanted to avoid packing too many outrageous adventures with supernatural bad guys into too short of a time period (averting that afore-mentioned "Murder, She Wrote Conceit" which others have referred to as "Cabot Cove Syndrome." But I realized there likely could be a few other adventures Michael might have that are a bit more mundane, and a bit shorter. Similar to the interactions Michael has with a whole cast of characters in the original 10,000-word short story "This Time Around" which later got re-adapted as the first few chapters in the full length first Michael Andrews or *Canadian Werewolf* novel.

One of my favorite movies of all time is *Planes, Trains and Automobiles*, the 1987 John Hughes film starring Steve Martin and John Candy. I enjoyed their cross-country misadventures. I reflected on how the movie lays out a series of unexpected side detours that happen on the journey. Which was like the things that distract Michael from moving forward and getting to where he needs to be in the short story *This Time Around*. (If you're unfamiliar with it, the premise is that he wakes up naked in Battery Park in Manhattan and realizes he is going to be late for an important meeting. He has to find some clothes, and get back to Midtown; but along the way he keeps encountering people who need his help; and his personal code of power and responsibility keep delaying his forward progress). Incidentally, this theme was something I explored in the very first short story I had ever published. "The Progressive Sidetrack" which appeared in print in 1992, was about a teenager wanting to ask the girl he has a crush on to go to a dance with him; but circumstances keep preventing him from getting to her in order to ask. Interestingly, the senior high school writing teacher I wrote the initial version of that story for told me it reminded her of the movie *Ferris Bueller's Day Off*, another John Hughes film. It's as if two of my biggest influences as a storyteller might just be John Hughes and Stan Lee.

In any case, I thought it might be fun to send Michael on a cross-country train ride, and throw a few obstacles in his way, preventing a straight-forward journey. I mean, what's the fun in that? I imagined that one roadblock in his way would come in the guise of someone who needs help, and a non-supernatural "bad guy" to face.

I wondered if it might be interesting being stuck on a train and about to turn into a wolf. How would Michael deal with that? Would he actually be a stow away on a train? And where was he going? And why?

I'm not sure where, or how Stowe, Vermont came into play. It might have been when I was consulting full-day train trips leaving Manhattan. But I was suddenly infatuated with the idea of titling the story "Stowe Away" because I liked the play on words (it matched the title twist idea of the novel length adventures), so I made the destination Stowe, Vermont. Then I needed a reason for his trip, and perhaps a companion or two for him to befriend along the way.

Heading north to help Gail because she was there for a family emergency and needed a friend was a perfect reason. It would show Michael's never-ending and unrequited love for Gail, an element from the novel that kept many readers turning the pages; and it would make sense in the continuing of that storyline that gets ratcheted up in a big way in the planned second full-length novel, the Los Angeles one. This also allowed me to explore more of Gail's back story and her family.

And then I needed to draw up some of the people he would encounter on his cross-country trip.

Bridget was meant to be one of many folks Michael helped. But as soon as I started drawing up her character, and the reason she was running, hiding on the train, she began to grow on me. And creating a unique bond between her and Michael, a combination friendship and father-daughter style relationship, drawing upon Michael's wolfish nurturing pack instincts, everything fell into place.

As I was developing Bridge, her character began to grow in further dimensions than I had originally intended. I love when characters do that to me. She demanded that she wouldn't merely be a victim on the run, but that she would actually help Michael as much as he helped her, that she wouldn't just be a protégé, she would be a mentor. She would help him, save him, protect him, and even advise him on his relationship with Gail.

And Bridget revealed all those things to me as I was writing the dialogue between her and Michael.

Sometimes, that magic happens when you put two characters in a room together and just get them to talk to one another.

Of course, Bridge is another one of those characters who has taken hold of me and won't let go. Because of how much I admire her, I suspect that she'll come back into Michael's life at some point.

I also admire at how, when I was trying to describe this story to someone, I said that it was like a cross between *Planes, Trains and Automobiles* and *Logan*, the 2017 film starring Hugh Jackman as Wolverine, where the superhero with extra-sensory abilities (similar to Michael) escorts a young girl to deliver her to a destination where she'll be safe from those who are tracking her.

The original draft of this story came to a little over 22,000 words. Deanna and Jamie helped me edit it down to approximately 17,000 words. At that length, it was still more than just a short story. It was, technically, a novella.

And, as such, I figured it should be book 1.5 in my Canadian Werewolf series. Nestled directly between book 1 (*A Canadian Werewolf in New York*), and book 2 (*Fear and Longing in Los Angeles*).

At the point I was planning all this out, I realized I needed to re-imagine the original cover for book 1, as well as the introductory 10,000-word short story "This Time Around." That resulted in establishing the series brand as Canadian Werewolf, and a consistent look and feel.

Because I was also motivated to get back to work on the other stories in the Canadian Werewolf universe that

I've been merely scratching at distractedly for the past few years.

And so, while I was at it, I had the covers for the existing books re-done, I had the cover for this one created, and I also commissioned the covers for the Los Angeles novel and the next planned short story written.

As I write this, I'm planning another short story for a different themed *Amazing Monster Tales* edition. That one is called *Monsters in Love* and for that I'll be exploring the back-story of how Michael and Gail met. Their meet cute (or "meat-cute" as one of my podcast listeners jokingly misheard me say). That one will be called *Lover's Moon* and will likely run in the 10,000 to 15,000-word range.

In parallel, I commissioned the narrator who was the voice of Michael Andrews for the audiobook version of "This Time Around," Scott Overton, to narrate this book, as well as begin work on the New York novel.

And I'm truly hoping that the forward momentum and investment, and the time spent back in Michael Andrews' world, will be the thing that propels me forward into getting that second full-length novel completed and then exploring what's next.

Of course, you, dear reader, will be the ultimate judge of how I did with that.

In the meantime, so as not to leave you hanging, I'll close this book with a bit of the teaser of the as-of-yet unedited opening for *Fear and Longing in Los Angeles*.

Mark Leslie
July 2020

Sneak Peek of Next Book: Fear & Longing in Los Angeles

On the following pages is a sneak peek of Book 2 in the *Canadian Werewolf* Series which takes place a couple of years after the events in this novella

Please note that, because this is the preview of an unedited first draft, there are likely to be edits/changes in the final text of the completed book. Also, there are still notes, often appearing in [square parenthesis] appearing in this text, usually with details meant to be filled in later.

Monday July 3, 2017

Prologue: I See a Full Moon Rising, I See Trouble on the Way

MICHAEL ANDREWS SHUDDERED at the words of the flight attendant on the overhead speaker, because it meant he was trapped with no way off of the plane now.

"Please be advised that we will be delayed for another hour here while waiting for ATC clearance on our revised schedule, and where we can fit into the takeoff que. This is a reminder to remain in your seats with your seatbelts fastened. We also remind you that all of your larger electronic personal devices should be stored in the overhead bins or under the seat in front of you. Your smaller devices, which you can store in the seat pockets in front of you, should be set to airplane mode."

He shifted uncomfortably, feeling the hot beads of sweat pouring down his forehead and his shirt soaking up the clamminess of his back.

No, this wasn't possible. It couldn't be happening.

He knew he should have gotten off the plane earlier, during that first flight delay, when they were still parked at the gate and hadn't closed the doors. But the first delay was only fifteen minutes, waiting for a crew member who was late via a delayed connecting flight. The second, while they were still at the gate, waiting for Air Traffic Control clearance, was only another half hour. The third delay, which they didn't specify, was another forty minutes. But this latest delay, an additional hour, this was pushing it too far.

He glanced out the window at the sun as it was making its descent slowly towards the hills in the western sky.

Even though he was traveling east, it would most certainly be nightfall while he was in the air.

The nightfall of a full moon. Okay, not the full moon, yet, but one that would be more than ¾ full.

And he had absolutely no control over the change. In the many years since his lycanthropic affliction, he never had control. During the cycle of the full moon his body morphed completely from human and into the full four-legged form of a wolf whenever the moon was at least ¾ full.

He turned to his companion, looked deep into her light green eyes. She stared back at him, placed her hand comfortingly on top of his.

"This isn't good," he whispered.

Tuesday June 13, 2017

CHAPTER ONE: What you Need is What You Need, or What

"WHAT YOU NEED is to get your head out of your ass," Mack said, slamming both of his hands down on the mahogany desk.

I regarded the man who I equally respected, loved, and feared as he kept his hands planted on the desk and flicked his head side to side in short, back and forth twitch-like movements.

For an obscure moment I reflected on how often I saw the man's head move like that – an odd little bobble-head type of motion, except side to side rather than up and down – and wondered if that was why he had such a small pencil-thin moustache above his top lip. A thicker moustache would match those thick bushy eyebrows, but I worried if it might fly off his face with the constant rapid motion he made when expressing his instant displeasure to something. Mack regularly displayed his displeasure in that fashion. Subtlety was not in his repertoire. It always amused me how, with his dark and bushy eyebrows and black and grey square headed buzz-cut, if he did have a full thick moustache it might make him look like J. Jonah Jamieson from the Spider-Man comic books.

Of course, whenever he was yelling at me, like he was doing right now, in his Manhattan office, I couldn't help but think of him as the angry head of the Daily Bugle, cursing and yelling across the desk at Peter Parker. Yes, even though I'm a fully grown adult and have been for several years, I still like to fantasize about being one of the heroes I've enjoyed reading about my entire life – particularly apt since, like Parker, I live in New York, and, several times in the past half dozen years, have used my special abilities to "fight the bad guys" or "fight crime" or "bring truth, justice and the American way" to the people. No, scratch that last one. I think that might be Superman, rather than Spider-Man. And I definitely don't live in Metropolis, wherever that is).

Mack Halpin – known in literary circles as "Mack the Knife" – my agent, was a hell of a tough nut, a complete hard-ass, difficult to reason with, and he often inspired most people he spoke with to want to either punch him in the face, or liberally apply a strip of duck tape across his lips. I suppose there were other reactions people could have, such as turning and walking away. But Mack didn't just express his opinion and desire; he infiltrated it into another person, got completely under the skin and could not, would not be ignored. Most folks would quickly classify Mack as an asshole; and in several ways I suppose he was. But he was also, perhaps the best thing to happen to my writing career. He took me under his wing, introduced me to opportunities that most writers only dream of and fought harder for me than I ever fought for myself.

If it weren't for Mack I wouldn't have had all of the amazing opportunities I've had in the past half dozen years, such as being a guest on *Late Night with David Letterman* in the final year before Letterman retired, having the New York Times run a weekly series about me every Saturday for a month, not to mention the fact my Maxwell Bronte novels hadn't just been optioned for screen rights, but one of them, *Print of the Predator*, had been made into a feature film starting Ryan Gosling, and another one [INSERT TITLE HERE] was currently in production, with Gosling back in the title role; and for both films, Mack had negotiated my own involvement as a junior executive producer. Of course, that didn't mean more than a bit of money in my pocket and a credit that scrolls by on the big screen at the end of the film, but it was yet another feather in my cap as a writer.

Like I said, I respected him. I loved how he looked after me the way a father would look after a rebellious teenage son; but the man also scared the bejesus out of me. He could be slightly amusing when going off on a rant; but he could also be a terrifying foe if you crossed him.

Heck, even with my enhanced strength, speed and sensory abilities which get progressively stronger the closer I am to the full moon phase of those monthly cycles, thanks to the lycanthropic curse running through my veins, Mack would likely be a challenging foe. Perhaps that was because he never pulled his punches and was prepared to fight dirty – whatever it takes – in order to win the fight.

That is why I was so thankful that he was fighting for me.

Well, most of the time.

Today, as he would sometimes do, he was fighting with me. Or, rather, that stubborn part of me that my logical mind couldn't over-power.

I stared across the desk at him, waiting, patiently, for the back and forth twitching of his head to stop. At times like now, it was difficult to supress a mirth-filled grin while waiting for that movement to cease, and I wondered if this habit of Mick's could be parlayed into a perpetual motion machine, like those novelty drinking birds that continued to bop up and down as if going back for more drinks of water.

"For the past two and a half years you have been moping around here like a pathetic love-sick teenager," Mack said. "I get it that she is a sweet piece of ass, but the world is filled with plenty of other juicy little asses. And you, my friend, looking like you do and with the stink of fame upon you, have a line up of women at your feet.

"I should know, half of the panties that get mailed to you come via this office. Hell, if they ever wanted to re-open Hogs and Heifers down in the meat-packing district with a ceiling of women's underwear, all I'd have to do is forward your fan mail for about a month."

My fingers dug into the arms of the chair to hear Mack use such a derogatory term to refer to Gail, the only woman that I had ever loved. Yes, I felt like a jerk for not standing up to such a slight, but one has to be strategic in when, where and how they argue with Mack.

I suppose this means that, as liberated as some men like to believe we have become regarding sexism and the objectification of women, we still have plenty of faults. Acknowledgement of the issue, of course, is always the first step towards resolving it, I suppose.

And, besides, I knew the signs, even without my extra-sensory ability to gage the man's underlying mood and intents based on his scent and his elevated heartbeat. I'd known Mack long enough to recognize that he was going off on a rant. And the best thing to do when that happens, as Cousin Eddy advises Clark Griswold in *Christmas Vacation* about the dog, Snots, who has a bit of Mississippi Leg Hound in him, should the dog ever be caught in the right mood and start going to town on your leg if he does lay into you, it's best to just let him finish.

"Not once in the years I have known you have you ever taken any of these women up on their blatant sexual offers. And let me tell you, son, that you're in dire need of a good fuck. I don't understand why you're such a damn prude about the whole thing.

"Man, if it were me, I'd be all over those women like a cheap suit.

"But no, you're all moony-eyed over Gail."

Mack had been gesturing wildly as he was speaking from behind his desk. But at this point he got up and started pacing back and forth between the desk and the plate glass window that offered a breathtaking view of the lower west side of Manhattan.

"She told you, point blank, son, exactly where you stand. Shit, she told you this more than once in the past couple of years. And yet you continue to let some idiotic romantic notion keep you from seeing what is right in front of your face."

I stopped looking at Mack and glanced down at my shoes. I knew he was right. Hearing it made me angry. Angry at him. Angry at myself. Angry at the situation.

But never angry at Gail.

I had, ultimately, caused this.

Meeting Gail was one of the best things that had ever happened to me. We hit it off almost immediately, drawn almost instinctively to one another. And in an extremely short time our lives swirled together in a wondrous ballet of physicality, sensuality, intellect and emotion. We seemed perfect for one another, connecting in all the important ways on so many incredible levels.

I had, truly, never experienced love in the way that I had with Gail.

And I knew, when our eyes first locked together, that I had found my soulmate, the one person I was destined to be with.

But I was ultimately, the reason our relationship ended.

More specifically, it was the lycanthropy. The werewolf curse running through my veins.

Despite the intimate sharing we experienced, I had kept the fact I was a werewolf from Gail. I mean, how does one explain to their sexual partner that for several nights during the cycle of the moon, their normal human body morphs into that of a wolf; and during that time, the human consciousness pretty much disappears, being replaced entirely by the alter-ego consciousness of a canine beast.

I didn't have to check the various dating books, or websites. I didn't need to consult with Mrs. Manners on the matter. I knew, quite simply, that there was no proper way to explain such a thing.

So I kept it hidden.

And, after we had been together for 3 full weeks, when the full moon phase was about to have its effect on me, I made excuses why we couldn't be together, why I had to be elsewhere. Gail was, understandably, confused, but accepted my feeble excuses.

But then, the following month, I had to do it again.

Then again.

And again.

I mean, how could I risk turning into a wolf and harming her in any way? I couldn't. There were things, back then, that I simply didn't know about my wolfish nature – so I simply could not take that chance.

And yes, despite Gail's background as the owner of a shop that specialized in the occult and paranormal, and her open mind, I just couldn't bring myself to admit this affliction that had affected me.

Perhaps I was afraid of rejection.

But rejection was what I ultimately received.

Gail knew I had been hiding something, and since I couldn't bring myself to share that intimate part of myself with her, she suspected I had been stepping out in the relationship. She had been burned badly before with infidelity and believed she had seen the signs of that again with my deception and excuses to not be with her during certain moments.

So the relationship ended. Or, rather, Gail ended the relationship.

And I had been a wreck about it for the longest time.

But then, one day, just a little over a year after she had dumped me, she came back into my life as a friend with two pieces of stunning news: She knew I was a werewolf; and she was engaged.

She had returned to my life to ask for my help in tracking down her fiancé whom she believed had been kidnapped. She'd known that I possessed extra-sensory perceptions, even when in human form, and that those senses were strongest closest to the cycle of the full moon.

She was an adept woman; intuitively picking up these subtle clues about my nature.

Of course, prior to me and even post me, she hadn't been all that good at choosing men.

Because we had learned, in the course of my investigation into his disappearance, that he had actually been unfaithful to her.

Given our mutual attraction and respect for one another, Gail and I remained friends.

Although, admittedly, I had wanted more. I had always wanted more.

And Gail had recognized that. Perhaps because I could sometimes be as subtle as a boisterous fart in a library.

Her insistence on not becoming close, not being more than friends continually broke my heart. But I always considered just having her in my life to be a special privilege; and reasoned that, at the very least, I could still have that.

But it did hurt. Having her so close and yet so far at the same time, continued to burn at the very fiber of my soul.

And, as usual, Mack was stone cold correct. He knew that the situation was killing me. He knew it was taking its toll on me. He knew that I most certainly wouldn't do anything about it, and that, if the situation were to be resolved, he would have to step in.

"Listen," Mack said. "She came back into your life when?"

"About two and a half years ago," I mumbled, still staring at my feet.

"And you had the ill-fated conversation about the possibility of re-kindling the romance when?"

"About two years ago."

"And what did she make absolutely clear to you?"

I hated that Mack was doing this; but a part of me was already starting to feel the benefit of the cross-examination approach to this therapeutic talk.

He took a step forward and in a louder voice asked it again. "What did she make absolutely clear to you?"

"That she wasn't interested in a relationship."

"Ahh," he said, holding a finger in the air, and I could swear he was imagining that we were in a courtroom. He paced a slow path behind his desk parallel to the window and looking out the window at the magnificent view of the city he repeated part of that back to me, or, perhaps, to the imaginary jury who were listening in. "She wasn't interested in a relationship.

"That is rather curious, isn't it? She was in your life again, but she was not interested in a relationship. What, pray tell, was she interested in?"

"Friendship."

He nodded his head, paced back along the window again. "Friendship." He nodded his head again and repeated the word. "Friendship.

"And so, what have you been to one another for the past two years?"

"Friends."

"That's all? Not 'friends with benefits'" Mack paused in his pacing to lean on his desk, his big bushy eyebrows lifting high up on his forehead as if being pulled to their limits by some sort of marionette strings.

"No."

"Not even the smallest, one quick and simple moment of carnal pleasure, benefit?"

"No."

"So," Mack said, "she made it perfectly clear, quite early on in this return to your life, that she was here as a friend, and only a friend. And, as you admit, after you

expressed you wanted something more, she made it perfectly clear that she simply wasn't interested. Do I have
that correct?"

"You do."

"So tell me, Mister Andrews," and Mack came out
from behind the desk and leaned back against it with his
arms folded across his chest, "why it is that, with the facts
all laid out in front of us, I can clearly see that the woman
is not interested, and you still can't get your goddamn
head out of your goddamn ass."

At that point, he broke the courtroom lawyer charade
and went right back into full Mack mode.

"For god's sake, man, I've been watching you mope
around here like some lovesick little puppy for two full
years. You're even worse than the first time she dumped
you. Of course, at least back then, you'd had the pleasure
of getting your rocks off before she put a complete and
utter stop to that.

"And now, without even the pleasure of a fun little
nightcap and a quickie or even a hand-job in the back of
a cab, you're mooning after her like some pathetic little
cheese-eating high school boy.

"I normally wouldn't give a rat's ass about my top cli-
ent's personal life. But *this* has been affecting your work,
your production. And I have a vested interest to keep
your rocket moving up, my friend."

Mack unfolded his arms, walked back around to the
other side of the desk and sat down in his chair.

"What you need is to distance yourself from that hot
little lady, find a distraction from the rut that you've

worked yourself into, and focus on something else for a while. What you need is exactly what I have arranged for you." He reached down, opened up a drawer on the right side of his desk, plucked out an envelope and slid it across the desk at me.

I stared at the envelope.

"Go ahead," he said. "Open it."

I gingerly reached out and picked it up. The envelope wasn't sealed. I pulled out a full sheet of paper folded into thirds around an additional few pieces of paper. It was a package from the travel agency that Mack's office used; I immediately recognized the letterhead even through the thin paper. It was a return-trip ticket to Los Angeles.

"What's this?" I asked. "A getaway vacation?"

"Christ, no," Mack said. "A getaway vacation wouldn't be to LA. It would be to Aruba or Punta Cana or maybe somewhere in the south of Italy.

"You're going to LA, or, more, specifically, to Hollywood, because I have negotiated a more direct hands-on role into that of script consultant. You'll be working on the set of [INSERT TITLE HERE].

"God knows you need the distraction, you need to get away from Gail for a while, and if the gods are smiling upon us, you need to get laid so you can start thinking with that big ball of meat sitting atop your shoulders rather than the little head you keep tucked in your pants."

"But, Mack," I said, looking down at the date. My flight was booked for tomorrow. I was still on the tail end of my monthly cycle. I started doing quick calculations in my mind, because I wasn't sure the percentage of the full moon. I did know, through experience, that I only turned into a wolf on the nights where the moon was at 80% or more. I fumbled my phone out of my back pocket and into my hand, toggling the screens over to the moon app so I could check. "You know I don't take well to travel. We've been through that before."

"*I don't take well to travel,*" Mack said in a high-pitched mocking tone. "Christ, Andrews, do you hear yourself. You're whining like a pre-school toddler. It's not like I'm sending you on a sixteen-hour flight to Hong Kong. It's less than a five-hour flight. And what the hell are you consulting on that phone? Oh, I know, it must be an app for Hypochondriacs. Get over yourself, you damn snow-flake."

I glanced over at the ticket again as the app was loading up, noting the time of the flight. It was with United and left Newark at 10 AM. That gave me a bit of a sense of relief, knowing I wouldn't be in the air during a potential change. I didn't, after all, want to be the inspiration for an odd new *Wolves on a Plane* horror film franchise. But I still had to worry about changing into a wolf in a city where I didn't have a routine planned out; not like I did here in Manhattan.

"What the hell are you panicking about, Andrews?" Mack said. "They'll let you take your damn teddy bear with you. You don't need to worry about that."

The app finished its boot cycle. I thumbed in Los Angeles and hit the refresh button. The fourteenth, tomorrow, the moon would be at 76% of its cycle. I was safe. I let out an audible sigh of relief.

Mack, sitting behind his desk, just staring at me.

"Are we okay now, sugar?" he said in a condescending tone.

"What? Oh, yeah."

"Good. Now get the hell out of my office. I have a call coming in that I need to take. Anne will confirm the hotel booking and a few of the other details with you." Mack was referring to Anne Lee, the tiny woman who acted as his executive assistant, his personal assistant, his chauffeur, his whatever-he-needed right hand person. She was, basically, the Alfred to his Bruce Wayne, the Whalen Smithers to his Monty Burns. "She can also check to confirm they are using hypoallergenic pillows and sheets, a smoke and fragrant-free environment, a vegan, gluten-free, carb-free, sugar-free, fucking flavor free restaurant, or whatever the hell else your pansy ass little heart desires to make sure you are comfy and cozy."

I slipped my phone into my back pocket and stood up.

"Thanks, Mack,"

"Yeah, yeah," he mumbled, already flipping open a file folder on his desk and scanning through it, well on to the next task on his list. I suppose it was another frustrating thing about him that I actually admired; how he could easily compartmentalize appointments, people, situations, into neat little boxes, focus entirely, intensely and 100% on them in the moment, but then move on to the next one, completely abandoning any emotional attachment to the previous ones in the interest of focusing 100% on the task at hand.

As I walked over to the door to leave his office I wondered if I would be able to do that on this little trip that he had planned for me

I closed my eyes for a moment, picturing Gail's beautiful smile, the delightful twinkle in her eye and then I shook my head.

"Compartmentalize," I muttered. "Turn the page."

~

End of sneak peek

To be informed about the release of *Fear and Longing in Los Angeles* sign up for the Mark Leslie Newsletter at www.markleslie.ca

About the Author

MARK LESLIE is a writer, editor and bookseller who was born and grew up in Sudbury, Ontario, spent many years in Ottawa and Hamilton, Ontario and currently lives in Waterloo, Ontario.

When he's not writing, Mark attaches "Lefebvre" back onto his name and works as a writing and publishing coach and consultant. As Director of Self-Publishing and Author Relations for Rakuten Kobo between 2011 and 2017, Mark established Kobo Writing Life which represents between 10 and 18% of Kobo's weekly unit sales, larger than any of the major publishers.

A bookselling veteran for more than twenty years, Mark has worked at virtually every type of bookstore, has sat on the Board of Directors for BookNet Canada and also been President of the Canadian Booksellers Association. He has given talks across Canada and the United States, in London, Paris and Frankfurt on the bookselling, writing and publishing industry.

Mark can be found online at www.markleslie.ca.

Selected Works

Non-fiction paranormal:

- *Haunted Hamilton: The Ghosts of Dundurn Castle and Other Steeltown Shivers* (2012)
- *Spooky Sudbury: True Tales of the Eerie & Supernatural* (2013) – Co-written with Jenny Jelen
- *Tomes of Terror: Haunted Bookstores and Libraries* (2014)
- *Creepy Capital: Ghost Stories of Ottawa and the National Capital Region* (2016)
- *Haunted Hospitals: Eerie Tales about Hospitals, Sanatoriums and Other Institutions* (2017) – Co-written with Rhonda Parrish
- *Macabre Montreal: Ghostly Tales, Ghastly Events, and Gruesome True Stories* (2018) – Co-written with Shayna Krishnasamy

Fiction:

- *One Hand Screaming* (2004)
- *Evasion* (2014)
- *I, Death* (2016)
- *A Canadian Werewolf in New York* (2016)
- *Nocturnal Screams* (Short Fiction Series) (2017/2018)
- *Stowe Away* (2020)
- *Fear and Longing in Los Angeles* (2021)

Editor:

- *North of Infinity II* (2006)
- *Campus Chills* (2009)
- *Tesseracts Sixteen: Parnassus Unbound* (2012)
- *Fiction River 23: Editors' Choice* (2017)
- *Fiction River 25: Feel the Fear* (2017)
- *Fiction River 31: Feel the Love* (2019)
- *Fiction River 32: Superstitious* (2019)

CPSIA information can be obtained
at www.ICGtesting.com
Printed in the USA
LVHW080543190820
663571LV00019B/386